Kailey

by Amy
Goldman
Koss

American Girl

To Sweetie!

Published by Pleasant Company Publications
Text copyright © 2003 by Pleasant Company
Illustrations copyright © 2003 by Philip Howe
Printed in China
03 04 05 06 07 08 C&C 10 9 8 7 6 5 4

Visit our Web site at **americangirl.com**

The characters and events portrayed in this book are fictitious. Any similarity to real persons, living or dead, is coincidental and not intended by the author.

Picture Credits: p. 143–Courtesy of Talia Hancock; p. 144–Courtesy of Talia Hancock; p. 145–© David Muench/CORBIS; p. 146–Courtesy of Talia Hancock; p. 147– © Pat O'Hara/CORBIS.

Library of Congress Cataloging-in-Publication Data
Koss, Amy Goldman, 1954–
Kailey / Amy Goldman Koss : [cover and story illustrations by Philip Howe].
p. cm.   "American Girl Today."
Summary: Ten-year-old Kailey launches an art protest to keep a developer from spoiling the cove and its tide pools that are specail to her and her family and friends.
ISBN 1-58485-591-6
[1. Real estate development–Fiction. 2. Seashore–Fiction.
3. Environmental protection–Fiction. 4. Tide pools–Fiction.
5. California–Fiction.] 1. Title. 2. Howe, Philip, ill.
PZ7.K8527Kai 2003   [Fic]–dc21   2002191246

Contents

Chapter 1: Moo-vies! 1

Chapter 2: Ouch! 17

Chapter 3: Ta-ta, Tide Pools 30

Chapter 4: Think! Think! 47

Chapter 5: Bummer, Dude 63

Chapter 6: A Done Deal 86

Chapter 7: Lemon Squares 104

True Story 142

1

Moo-vies!

My best pal, Tess, grabbed her boogie board and started climbing down the cliff ahead of me. From where I watched, she looked like a weird bug, crab-walking on the rocks. I stopped to take a deep breath of California's salty-fishy sea air. Ah! My favorite smell.

Tess yelled, "Come on, Kailey!"

So I grabbed my gear and started down.

"No trips to the hospital today, girls!" Dad called after us. That's his way of reminding us to be careful.

At the bottom of the cliff, I ran across the sand to the boulder where we always leave our stuff. There were millions of seagull and sandpiper footprints, but

Tess's and mine were the first human prints of the day. I love that.

I caught up with Tess and dug a nickel out of my pocket. "Call it!" I said.

She called, "Heads!"

Tails—I won. That meant we'd visit our "friends" in the tide pools first. If it had landed on heads, we would have gone into the water first. Tess and I are both crazy about bodyboarding and snorkeling, but Tess doesn't love snooping around the tide pools as much as I do.

We crawled out to the far rocks, the ones that stuck way into the water. Out there, every little pock and hole fills and refills with each splashing tide.

They were all there—the sea anemones who shrink back and squirt when you touch them, small snails with pretty patterned shells, red clams, and purple barnacles. I didn't see any starfish, but one tide pool had a sand dollar.

I'm a normal-sized ten-year-old girl, but standing

over the pools, I feel gigantic. Each pocket in the rocks is like a tiny water world of its own, a perfect mini aquarium. And there was my shadow, big enough to cause instant night for the creatures who lived there!

A brave, itty-bitty crab scurried up on a rock to wave his front claw at me. I waved back. "Hello to you too, Mr. Crabby," I said.

SWOOSH! A wave snuck up and sprayed without warning. It whisked some of the tide-pool creatures back out to sea, including Mr. Crabby. Bye!

Now a smooth gold snail shell was slowly sinking to the bottom of the freshly filled pool.

Tess was soaked and sputtering. The wave must have caught her bending down with her mouth open.

I held my hands up megaphone style and yelled, "Surf's up!" at the ocean.

When we got back to our boulder, Dad was setting up his easel and getting his tubes and brushes ready. My dad paints seascapes for greeting cards and calendars and things like that. He smiled at me and Tess and said, "Gorgeous enough for you?"

I looked around and he was right, the day was twinkly and bright, with no haze and no crowds. Then I half-noticed something poking out from behind the rocks. I looked harder. That's when I saw the corner of the sign. I climbed over the rocks and ran across the sand to take a look. It said:

COMING SOON!
Commercial Cove Resort
Phase One
An Exclusive Oceanfront Entertainment Experience!

Huh? I thought. *Here?*

The sign showed a tall, supermodern building towering over the bluff. It looked so weird, so out of place. I laughed, thinking it was like seeing a whale on ice skates or a moose on a surfboard. Because from where I stood, not only couldn't I see anything resort-like, I couldn't see anything at all besides sky, water, and rock. There wasn't a single trace of civilization. No buildings, telephone poles, cars . . . nothing.

Looking closer at the picture on the sign, I saw that there was not only the hotel part but also a shopping mall with a bunch of stores and restaurants and a movie theater multiplex with twelve screens. And there was a wide staircase coming down the cliff, all the way from the hotel-mall building to the beach.

Cool! I thought. No more scrambling down rocks to get here. Better yet—no crawling back up, carrying heavy, wet gear when we're tired.

The picture also had some kind of snack bar thingie down on the beach. WOW! We could just run across the sand for lunch! That would be totally awesome, and way easier than lugging our own coolers and water bottles up and down. And HEY, they might even have a bathroom!

Tess had run up behind me and now she was cheering and leaping around. "Kailey!" she shrieked. "Can you believe it? TWELVE movie theaters! Isn't it fantabulous? Fan-TAB-u-lous!" She grabbed my hands and swung me in circles.

I'm not the movie addict that Tess is, but I started to laugh anyway. Around and around we spun until she let go and I went flying. I landed in a heap. But when I lunged after her, she darted away chanting, "Moo-vies! Moo-vies! Moo-vies!"

Meanwhile, my dad had come over and was reading the sign.

"Is that great or what?" Tess giggled, trying to catch her breath.

"Or what," Dad answered seriously. "VERY or what." He sure didn't seem excited. But Tess laughed and went cartwheeling off, kicking up sand in huge arches.

Back at our boulder, I tied my hair in a knot and

started wiggling into my wet suit and water socks. Dad slowly came back to his easel. He looked gloomy, but when I asked him what was wrong, he just patted me on the head and said, "Go enjoy the water." Then, instead of getting to work, he sat down and dug his feet into the sand.

I knew it was the sign that had upset him, because he'd been acting normal until he saw it. It's kind of weird that the same sign could make Tess so happy and Dad so UNhappy.

Tess slid her boogie board out of its bag and strapped the leash to her wrist. I looked back toward the sandy part of the beach. The waves were breaking just right. I grabbed my board and raced her in.

By the time we got past the break, duck-diving through the waves, all thoughts of the sign or Dad's gloominess were gone. It's impossible to think or worry about anything when you're being tossed around by the waves. At least for me. From the first icy blast and salty splash, my eyes pop open, my skin tingles, and I suddenly feel totally AWAKE! Everything but the sound of the surf is washed right out of my head.

And once I slide my belly onto that board and lift off on the crest of a wave coming in, I feel like a leaf, like a feather, like nothing at all! And after I've been clobbered by a few waves and tossed around in the bubbly white water, my head is as clear and wide and empty as the sky.

Tess loves to just float along on her board, bobbing with the waves. I like that too, but the best part for me is the ride, the exciting splash, crash, spray-on-my-face flying! Actually, I like the paddling out, too. Even those bouncy rides that practically shake my teeth loose are fun in their own way. I don't even mind taking a spill and ending up with a mouth full of sand. It's all fun.

I'm not saying that I should have been born a mermaid, but I can't imagine what life would be like without the ocean and the beach. My mom is a

marine microbiologist. Now she just sits in a window-less lab, miles from the sea, staring at her computer screen. But when she was pregnant with me, Mom was doing research aboard a ship. She thinks that's why I love the ocean so much. She says those months made the rhythm of the tide as natural to me as it would be to a fish.

Plus, Dad has been taking me along with him to different beaches since I was tiny. My earliest baby memories are of looking way up from the sand at his paintbrush moving far above me.

Anyway, Tess and I caught one amazing ride after another. Some were peeling so long and high that I felt like I was part of the water itself. Some friends of ours from school—Mandy, Destiny, and Chloe—paddled out to join us and we all rode the waves together, which was a blast. At one point, all of us were waiting way out past the break when a whole huge flock of pelicans landed in the water around us. We all bobbed together in a flock like old friends.

When Dad gave me and Tess the hand signal to come in, it felt like no time at all had passed. But as we hauled ourselves out of the water, I shivered in the colder air and noticed that the sun was way lower in the sky.

There'd be no time to snorkel today. No spying on the secret world of fish. *Oh well,* I thought, *there's always tomorrow, and tomorrow's tomorrow.* After all, summer vacation had just begun, and there were endless, glorious beach days ahead!

Tess and I ran dripping over to Dad. I was shocked to see that he hadn't painted a single stroke! That reminded me of the sign, so I went back to check it out again.

I took my time and looked closely. In the picture, the blue lounge chairs and umbrellas dotting the beach were pretty, but something seemed wrong. What was it?

Tess came up next to me to chant, "Moo-vies, moo-vies," in my ear.

I stared at the sign some more until I finally realized what was so strange: in the picture, the beach was drawn as one long curve of white sand.

"Hey!" I said. "This isn't our beach." I pointed at the drawing. "Look! There are no tide pools or rocks on the shore. They must be building this somewhere else."

"WHAT?" shrieked Tess.

"Well, look. The picture shows a sandy beach, not a rocky one."

"NO FAIR," Tess wailed. "I was all excited about those movie theaters being so close. I could TASTE the popcorn!" Then, with a huge sigh, she said, "I should have known it was too good to be true." Tess made a disappointed-frown face that cracked me up.

We packed our gear and went up to the car. The climb seemed harder than ever. I accidentally kicked some stones loose. They rained down in a mini avalanche on Tess, who was climbing behind me.

She dodged the little stones and grumbled nonstop. "Doesn't it just figure that the whole mall thing was just a mean trick? A tease? Can you stand it?" she asked. "And you know what? I bet Dee would have taken us shopping with her and her friends."

Tess's sister, Dee, isn't my all-time favorite teenager, but it is true that Dee lives to shop, and maybe she would have taken us along sometime—if her mom made her.

"Dee is going to be HEARTBROKEN when I tell her we ALMOST had a mall," Tess wailed. "Is this the worst of the worst, or what?"

• • •

We dumped all our stuff in the trunk of the car and went across the street to Fish King to get dinner.

"P.U.," Tess said. "It stinks in there. I'll wait outside."

But I love that store, so I went in with Dad. There was a long line, as always. The Hong brothers, who own it, are incredibly fast behind the counter, weighing and wrapping fish, zip-zap, remembering practically every customer's name and taste. They know we are salmon and shrimp people.

One of my dad's paintings hangs on the wall over their display of mustards and marinades. It's a storm scene, with the waves all blown out and a few gulls racing for land across a yellow-gray sky. I think the painting is a little too chilly and a little too scary, but the Hong guys love it.

When it was our turn, Joe Hong wrapped up a salmon fillet that he said he'd been saving especially for us. Then he asked if Dad had heard about the cove.

Dad nodded sadly. Joe nodded sadly back.

"Wow!" I said. "News travels fast! We just now saw the sign."

Joe said, "Fast but not fast. We been fighting this forever! No luck. Big boys win and little man weeps."

"It will sure ruin your view," Dad said. But when we turned to look, the throng of people behind us was so thick, we couldn't even see the window. I thought that was funny.

Joe shrugged and said, "Man come in, offer us be their fish king, big bucks to supply them." I wondered if Joe meant the restaurant on the beach. Maybe they'd serve crab cakes or shrimp skewers down there. Yum!

Joe's brother Ed yelled from across the room, "Did you tell Pete about painting?" (My dad's name is Pete.)

"Oh!" Joe said, hitting his forehead. "Hotel man saw your painting. Big fan. Ask your phone number. Hope you don't mind we gave it to him. OK?"

Now it was Dad's turn to shrug. Customers in line behind us were getting annoyed, so Dad paid for our fish and we left.

I had a million questions, and I asked them as soon as we got into the car. Here's what I learned: Joe and his brothers and the other owners of little stores on the bluff have been trying to keep the Commercial Cove resort-hotel-movies-mall thing from being built. They are afraid it will drive them out of business. Dad explained, "Some people would rather shop in a mall than in town."

"Me!" Tess said. "I would for sure!"

"There you go," Dad said, smiling at Tess.

Tess beamed, but then her face fell. "But what about it being the wrong beach—the no-rocks thing?"

"Rocks can be moved," he said.

I laughed, sure that he was kidding. We aren't talking about pebbles here, and we're not even talking about a few boulders. We're talking about tons and tons of humongous, gigantic rocks.

"Oh, sure," I said. "Like someone would MOVE the tide pools!"

But Dad didn't laugh. He didn't even smile. I wasn't sure what to think about that, but I noticed that Dad barely said another word all the way home.

2

Ouch!

Mom came home while Tess and I were standing around the barbecue grill watching Dad. He is very particular about his barbecue.

"Thirty-six charcoal briquettes!" he insisted.

"Not thirty-five?" Tess teased.

He looked horrified.

"What happens if you use thirty-seven?" I asked.

"Then the salmon's ruined and we have to eat out," said Mom, giving Dad a peck on the cheek.

"None of you shows proper respect for the chef!" Dad huffed, pretending to sulk.

Tess asked my mom if she'd heard about the resort-movies-mall building on the cove.

Mom looked at Dad. "We lost?" she asked him.

He nodded. "There's a sign up, so I guess it's official. They refer to it as—get this—'Commercial Cove Resort, An Exclusive Oceanfront Entertainment Experience,' unquote."

Mom laughed. "It's kind of funny in an awful, terrible way," she said.

Tess put her fists on her hips. "Hey, what's so awful-terrible about hotels and movies and shopping?"

"Not a thing," Mom said. "It's just that there's a place for everything, and we don't think our cove is the place for an eighty-eight-room hotel or a twelve-screen multiplex."

"And every starfish and sea urchin in the tide pools agrees with us," Dad added.

Tess looked from one to the other and shook her head. I could tell she thought my parents were nuts.

"You know," Tess said to me on our way to my room, "I don't think your family likes change."

I looked around the living room. The furniture

was exactly the same as it had been in my earliest baby pictures. I giggled and said, "I think you're right."

• • •

Later Tess handed me her brush. I knew what that meant. Whenever Tess sleeps over, she wants me to braid her hair into ninety zillion tiny braids so it'll dry all wavy by morning. My hands get tired, but she pays me back by telling me stories the whole time.

This time, she said she'd tell my fortune.

"Since when do you know how to tell fortunes?" I asked her.

"I was secretly trained, in a top-secret way, by one of my ancient secret relatives," explained Tess.

She couldn't have meant her grandparents or her aunts or uncles, because I knew all of them and they were not the ancient secret type. But I said, "OK, ready."

"Spirits," Tess said, putting on her ghost-story voice, "tell us what Kailey's life will be like when she's older."

"Exactly like it is now," I answered for the spirits. Tess shushed me. Then she made her voice spookier and said, "O spirits, answer my question!"

"They don't have to answer," I said. "I already did. My life is going to stay the same, I hope."

Tess dropped her fortune-teller act and said, "Seriously? You're not just dying to grow up?"

"Eeew, no!" I answered. "It looks gross and boring. Well, all right, I'd like to be big enough to wax up a real surfboard and ride the monster waves in Hawaii, but otherwise my life is fine just how it is."

"Aw, come on," Tess said.

"Why?" I asked. "What do you think is going to be so great?"

Tess said, "Everything! Making my own money. Driving. Staying out late. Eating junk food whenever I want to. Seeing all the movies I want, no matter how they're rated. Just EVERYTHING!"

I rolled my eyes.

"No, really," Tess insisted. "I'm going to be a

movie star–slash–supermodel, and I'll wear great clothes and makeup and tons of jewelry and cool shoes with ten-inch heels, and I'll have my own apartment and my own phone and lots of fantabulous parties, and I'll dye my hair as many colors as I want to whenever I want! Every girl on the planet will be totally green with envy!"

"I won't be," I said.

"Aw, come on, Kailey! Don't you want to be driven around in a mile-long limousine?" Tess whined.

I reminded her that I get carsick. "And anyway, I thought you wanted one of those little sports cars that look like they've been sat on by elephants."

"That too!" Tess laughed. "But seriously, Kailey, we can't just play in the sand our whole lives."

"Can too!" I said. "Just watch me!" But I knew Tess was probably right. *Ick.*

The next morning, we went back to the cove with my parents, but when we looked down this time, the water was full of swimmers and surfers and boogie boarders. The sand was covered with blankets and umbrellas, and even from the top of the cliff, the smell of sunblock and lotion was stronger than the smell of the sea.

I was disappointed, but that's the way weekends are around here: CROWDED. So, forget the snorkel gear—we'd be lucky if we could even board without being rammed by bigger kids.

"There're always the tide pools," I said.

Tess nodded, but not very enthusiastically.

Mom was wearing her wide-brimmed hat and carrying a sack full of work stuff and towels. I knew she'd sit in the shade of a big old rock, clicking away on her laptop all day without ever getting wet.

Dad grabbed his sketchbook and charcoal pencils instead of his paint box. That meant we weren't going to stay as long. Bummer. My idea of a perfect summer day was to get to the beach as soon as the sun came up and stay there as long as there was enough light to see by. But I didn't complain, because we had the whole summer ahead of us, and weekends would be just a small part of it.

I pointed the sign out to Mom and wondered how I could have missed seeing it yesterday when I'd looked down at the beach. It seemed so huge today, smack-dab in the center of the cove.

Tess was already on her way down. I grabbed my stuff and followed her. Dad called out, as usual, "Remember, the emergency room is extra crowded on weekends." Then he and Mom started down, too.

Each of us was concentrating on the rocks, think-ing our own thoughts, when suddenly Tess screamed and boom! She fell and slip-slid down the rocks—bam—hitting one rock, slam—against another! Tess bumped and tumbled, then jolted to a stop. For a split second there was total silence. That scared me out of my mind! But then Tess started screaming at the top of her lungs.

My parents and I scrambled down to her. Tess

was covered with gravel and tears and dirt, and she was all scraped up, but, thank goodness, there wasn't much blood.

Tess couldn't put weight on her right foot, so Dad scooped her up and carried her back to the top of the bluff. Mom and I crawled behind them, gathering strewn pencils and towels and calling, "Everything is going to be OK!" up to Tess.

Dad put Tess down on the hood of the car, and he and Mom looked her over. Then Mom got her cell phone out of the glove compartment and called Lynn, Tess's mom.

Lynn must have been pretty hysterical because my mom had to keep saying, "She's fine. No, not much blood. No, I don't think she hit her head," over and over until she hung up. Mom told Tess that her mom would be here in a second. And she was.

Her car screeched to a stop. The car door flew open and Lynn came barreling out. She grabbed Tess by the shoulders and kept asking, "Are you all right, Tessie? Are you all right?"

Then she helped Tess into the car, and off they zoomed.

My parents and I looked at each other. None of us were sure what to do next. It had all happened so fast. And now, except for the screaming seagulls, everything was so quiet.

Dad went back down to search the cliffside for the rest of our stuff. I guess we'd dropped everything and it had bounced all over the place—boogie boards, water bottles, papers, Mom's computer, Dad's charcoal pencils. I knew I should help, but I was too freaked.

Mom and I just leaned against the side of the car. Every few minutes she'd say, "Don't worry, Kailey. Tess will be fine." And I'd say, "For sure."

Or I'd say, "Tess is going to be OK," and Mom would answer, "Absolutely."

By then Dad had come up for the last time and he was ready to leave. We drove home in almost total silence for the second day in a row.

My parents and I sat around the house worrying about Tess and telling each other not to worry. I left about five hundred messages on Tess's answering machine. Finally, she called to say that my dad was right: the hospital's emergency room is extra crowded on weekends.

Tess said she was all banged up and covered with bruises. But most importantly, a bone in her foot was broken and she was in a cast! She said she'd have to stay off her foot for ages, and it hurt like crazy. She also told me that her mom wasn't going to let her go to the cove again until they'd put in an elevator. And her dad said she could only snorkel and boogie board in the bathtub from now until she turns twenty-one. I knew they were half-joking.

Dad made a quick card with a really cute drawing of Tess on it. Then, after dinner, my parents and I went over to see her.

Tess was in her bed, propped up on dozens of pillows and surrounded by her dolls and stuffed animals. The whole room smelled like nail polish because Tess's sister, Dee, was doing Tess's nails. That was pretty shocking since Dee isn't exactly the sweetest big sister in town.

Tess looked like a happy princess until I looked closer and saw that her cheek was scraped and her lip was swollen and purplish on one side. And then there was her foot, in a canary yellow cast, with the tips of her toes sticking out.

I was afraid for a minute that Tess would be in too much pain to act normal, but she smiled her big Tess smile when she saw me and said, "Hey, girl!"

I said, "Hey!" and sat down on the edge of her bed. Tess winced, pointing to her cast.

"Sorry!" I said. "Sorry, sorry, sorry!"

Tess said, "It's OK," but she moved her foot away.

"Really, Tess, I'm so sorry about all this. Does it hurt terribly?"

"Only when someone sits on it," Tess said, but I was pretty sure she was joking.

"Well, I feel so bad that it's going to ruin your whole summer and everything."

Tess lifted her chin bravely and said, "At least it got me a manicure!" She wiggled her pinkish orange nails at me. "Like the color?" she asked.

I nodded, and Dee said, "Want me to do yours?"

Huh? Dee had never spoken to me before except to say stuff like, "Get out of the bathroom," or "Forget about the peach yogurt. It's mine."

I shook my head. "No thanks."

Dee offered again! She said, "You sure, Kailey?"

Hey! Dee knew my name? After only four years of me and Tess being friends? I was practically speechless, but I managed to say, "Thanks anyway."

Dee almost SMILED at me! Then, without a single insult, she gathered up her tissues and cotton balls and swabs and bottles and left the room.

When we were alone, I said, "What's up with that? Dee was so nice!"

Tess said, "I know! I think she feels guilty about

all the times she's been rotten to me, now that I'm all wrecked and uglified."

"You're not ugly," I said.

"Am too," Tess said.

"Are not. It's all scrapes and stuff that will heal up."

"Yeah, but what am I supposed to DO meanwhile?"

"We'll think of something," I said. "Cross my heart!"

"'Course, I could go to movies all day and night, but the multiplex isn't built yet. I might as well be in school, for all the fun I'm gonna have this summer," she said, and she sounded as if she was about to cry.

I didn't know what to say. In all the time we'd been friends, I'd seen Tess cry exactly twice. And both times were during sad movies.

When my parents came in to say hi to Tess and coo over her cast, I was glad. And for the first time ever, I was glad when they said it was time to leave.

3

Ta-ta, Tide Pools

When I finally fell asleep that night, I had a really yucky nightmare about falling down the cliff and smashing like an egg. I woke up and shook off the dream, but when I fell back asleep, there it was again, yolk and all. I was more tired in the morning than I had been the night before.

By the time I came down for breakfast, Mom was already working at her computer. Dad asked me what I wanted to do today, and I automatically said, "Let's go to the beach."

He raised his eyebrows and said, "Really?"

"Really," I answered, although I felt a little guilty about Tess.

"Our home beach or another one?" he asked.

"Ours, of course!" I said. Any other beach would be a longer drive, and no beach was as familiar and homey. I loved every inch of our cove: every rock, every shell, every pebble, and every grain of sand.

But when we got there, I froze. I hadn't counted on how weird it would feel to look down from the top and see Tess fall again in my mind. I hadn't expected to hear her scream echo in my ears.

It was still early, so the beach wasn't all that crowded, but suddenly the thought of poking around in the tide pools all alone or boogie boarding without Tess seemed way too depressing.

Dad must have seen me freeze because he said, "Guess it's like falling off a horse. You gotta get right back on."

He started a little way down the cliff so I'd follow him—but I couldn't.

I said, "Let's just go home." So we did.

Mom was surprised to see us. She followed me

into my bedroom and said, "I guess the cove didn't look so good to you today."

"I know it's silly to blame the cliff for Tess's accident," I said, "but I can't help it."

Mom nodded.

"The rocks didn't trip her on purpose," I said.

"No, they didn't," Mom agreed.

"And we've gone up and down that cliff a zillion times," I said. "And none of us has ever fallen before. So it's not like now we're going to just tumble down all the time. Right?"

Mom nodded again. "Right."

"So what is it?" I asked.

Mom shrugged and pushed the hair out of my eyes.

"Maybe it's the sign," I said.

Mom didn't know what I meant, so I explained. "The 'Commercial Cove' sign. The 'Coming Soon!' The—what was it? 'Waterfront Adventure Experience' or something?"

Mom smiled. "Something like that. But I know it had the word 'exclusive' in there somewhere, meaning it's planning to *exclude* someone."

"Exclude? Like, leave out?" I asked.

Mom shrugged. "That's what 'exclusive' means. But people use it to mean ritzy or expensive."

"Well," I continued, "ever since I saw that exclusive sign, everything has been screwy."

"Imagine how the starfish and anemones would feel if they could read it," Mom said. "After all, they are the ones being most excluded."

I asked what she meant, and she said, "They plan to redesign the coast, which means dredging the ocean floor and hauling off the rock. Ta-ta, tide pools."

"Aw, come on," I said. "They can't really do that —can they?"

Mom nodded.

"But why would they even want to?" I asked, feeling all confused. "What does wrecking the tide pools have to do with hotels and movie theaters?"

Mom held her hands up in a helpless shrug. "I don't know. It's some big secret. Maybe they're going to drill for oil, but I doubt it. Maybe the developers are just anti-rock! Rock haters for some deep psychological rock-phobic reason. Who knows? My guess is that they think sharp, slippery rocks are dangerous and will make for lawsuits. Maybe they're afraid the tourists will trip and hurt themselves and will blame them," Mom said. "Commercial Cove Resort probably does not want to be sued."

"That's a totally stupid reason to dig up a whole tide-pool universe!" I said. "And it's so mean!"

"I agree," Mom said.

"So why don't we stop them?"

"We've been trying for years," Mom said. "Remember those community meetings in the rec center?"

Yes, I remembered being dragged along to meetings with my parents, but I'd always hung out in the back of the room waiting for the cookies and juice to be served. And when Tess and other kids from school were there, we played hide-and-seek or freeze tag outside.

"I didn't know those meetings were about saving the beach!" I said.

"Your father and I have been talking about it for over a year around the house, at the dinner table, in the car . . ." Mom said.

I shrugged.

"I always suspected that you don't listen to us, and now here's proof," Mom laughed. "But I thought you just didn't hear us when we asked you to clean your room!"

I blushed. I did kind of remember them talking about development and building and stuff like that, but it never occurred to me to wonder what all the fuss was about. I never thought it would have anything to do with me and my life. But the beach and the tide pools ARE my life!

Mom gave me a little hug. "Don't worry about it,

sweetheart. Even if you had been paying attention, there wouldn't have been anything you could have done to make a difference."

Then Mom asked if I'd like a ride over to Tess's house to visit her. She said we could stop at the bakery and bring Tess a treat. I jumped to my feet. I knew exactly which cookies we'd get. Tess's favorite.

Lynn was gardening when we got there. My mom plopped down next to her and started weeding. The moms have been great friends since Tess and I introduced them at school.

I went inside. Tess was looking through a stack of videotapes and didn't hear me come into her room.

"Hi, girl, wazzup?" I said.

Tess jumped and cracked a smile, but the swollen side of her face didn't smile as well as the other half did. "Oh, Kailey! I'm sooo glad you're here!" she wailed. "I'm bored to death!"

"I bet you are," I said. "I know I'd go nuts having

to sit around inside all the time."

"I guess I've kinda wrecked your summer, too," Tess said. "You probably hate me."

"I do not," I said.

"Do too."

"Not."

"Too," she said, but then she smiled.

I gave her the bakery box and sat down very carefully at the foot of her bed.

"White chocolate macadamia nut?" Tess squealed.

And I said, "Of course."

Tess tore open the box. She asked me what movie I wanted to watch.

"A funny one," I answered. "But first, I have to talk to you about something important."

"Like what?" she asked, shoving a cookie into her mouth.

"The tide pools."

"Well, I won't be seeing them for a while," Tess said.

"And the hotel-mall-resort-movie building," I added.

"I told Dee all about it, and she's as excited about it as we are," Tess said with her mouth stuffed full.

"Well, we have to think of a way to stop them from building it," I said.

"WHAT?" Tess said, spraying cookie crumbs across the bed. "Have you lost your mind, Kailey? That mall will be the best thing that ever happened to us!"

"And the worst thing that ever happened to Mr. Crabby and all the other little guys on the beach."

Tess said, "Huh?"

So I told her everything I knew about the tide-pool rocks being dragged away. "Rocks that have probably been there for millions of years," I said. "Including our boulder! Remember the picture on the sign?"

"No way," Tess said. "No one would do that."

"'Fraid so!" I said.

"'Fraid not." Tess thought hard for a second. Then she brightened up and said, "Well, if they are doing it, then it must be an OK thing to do or they wouldn't do it. And anyway, the ocean is a big place. I bet the tide-pool critters will just swim to some other rocky place."

"But this rocky place is their home!" I said.

"Aw, Kailey," Tess said, picking up a couple of videos. "Whenever anyone builds ANYTHING, it has to be somewhere! Even if it's out in the middle of an empty field, it's someone's home. Worms, bugs, groundhogs, whatever. Right?"

I said, "Right."

"Well, we get twelve movie theaters and a mall in exchange for Mr. Crabby! That's a primo deal! It could have been worse, ya know, much worse. They could be building something creepy, like a monster dentist's office, or a car-fixing place, or some pollution-stinky factory. We are totally lucky!"

"And there'll be stairs down to the beach," I agreed. "That'll make a big difference."

"No kidding," Tess said, pointing to her cast.

I knew that if the resort's stairs had been there, Tess wouldn't have tripped. *I suppose that's a fair trade,* I thought. *Tide pools for stairs and unbroken feet.*

Tess handed me a video and told me to pop it in, so I did. But I couldn't really concentrate. Something was still bugging me about the whole tide-pool thing.

Tess snickered as the cartoon cat got clobbered by the cartoon mouse. Tess looked like she'd been clobbered by a whole mob of mice. In fact, she looked more banged up today than she had last night.

I asked myself how I could look at my best friend, all bruised and swollen, and still not want the resort —even though I knew that once there were stairs, accidents like Tess's wouldn't happen.

Did that make me a bad friend? Wasn't it mean of me to be thinking about the happiness of clams and snails when poor Tess was locked inside watching dumb movies on such a perfect beach day? And not just today but tomorrow, too, and the next day, and as many days of her summer vacation as it'd take for her foot to heal?

I told myself that Tess deserved the mall and movie theaters since she wanted them so much. But I still felt that dragging away the tide-pool rocks just wasn't right.

"You know," I said over the sound of the cartoon, "once they take away the rocks, there won't be any more snorkeling."

Tess said, "What do you mean?"

"Well, all the fish come to hang out around the rocks. So if there're no rocks, there'll be no fish. At least no reef fish. No one really pretty."

Tess grabbed the remote and hit the pause button. She looked at me hard. "Kailey, what is your problem? We're getting a MALL. That's a good thing. And there's nothing you could do about it even if it was totally evil. So get over it, OK?"

"But . . ."

"But nothing," Tess said. "OK?"

∘ 41 ∘

I shrugged.

Tess rolled her eyes at me. Then she clicked the cartoon back on.

I ate one of her white chocolate macadamia cookies, although I'm really a plain-sugar-cookie kind of girl.

• • •

When Mom and I got home, Dad was pacing in the living room. He flung his arms in the air at the sight of us and opened his mouth to say something, but then he shut it again. He jammed his hands deep into his pockets instead and paced away again.

"What's going on?" Mom asked.

Dad whirled around to face us but didn't say anything.

Mom and I looked at each other.

Dad pulled his hands out of his pockets to rake them through his hair while he paced.

"Dad?" I said.

Mom said, "Pete?"

He finally answered. "I got a call."

"From?" Mom asked.

"The Man."

"What man?" I asked.

"The Commercial Cove Resort, Explorations in Extravagant Exclusion Man," he said.

Mom nodded. "Why did he call here?"

"You'd better sit down," Dad answered. So Mom and I sat.

"He wants to commission me to paint eighty-eight seascapes for the hotel rooms."

Mom gasped. "Eighty-eight paintings?"

Dad nodded. "And he wants me to do two murals, one in the lobby and one over the hotel bar."

Mom gasped again.

"He's seen my art around town, at Fish King and the diner. He thinks I capture the, quote, spirit of the cove, unquote."

"Well, he's right, you do," Mom said. "But yikes! Eighty-eight paintings? That's great. I mean, that's terrible. I mean, well, you know what I mean."

Dad smiled a crooked smile. "It would be an unbelievable amount of money." Then he grabbed his hair again and said, "On the other hand . . ."

Mom nodded and said, "I know."

Dad shoved his fists back into his pockets and began pacing the room again. His hair poked out in all directions.

I was totally confused. "This is good news, right?"

"It's not that simple," Mom said. "You know."

I said, "No, I don't know."

"Sure you do, Kailey," she said. "You know that if your dad helped the bad guys with their 'Adventures in Exclusion,' he'd be helping them to destroy our cove. Not directly, of course, but . . ."

"I might as well haul the tide pools away on my own back!" Dad said, pacing faster.

"But still," Mom said, "that's a lot of money. And a lot of money washes away a lot of worries."

My parents looked at each other with their eyes

wide. Then the next thing I knew, Mom was up and pacing, too.

I sat on the couch and watched them.

"It would be going over to the enemy side," Dad said.

"It would get rid of our credit card debt," said Mom. But then she added, "Nasty thought, though,

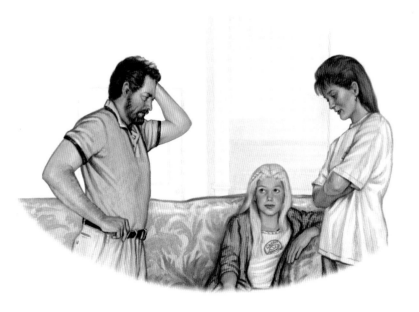

the idea of painting pictures of our beautiful beach to hang in the tall, ugly building that destroyed it."

"Right," Dad said. "So the tourists can see what the cove looked like before they crowded in with all their traffic and litter and noise."

He yanked his hands out of his pockets to claw at his hair again, saying, "But at least then we'd be able to afford to stay at the resort for a night or two."

"How long do you have before you have to tell him yes or no?" Mom asked.

"He's going to call back to set up a meeting. Just to talk. I don't think I have to have an answer yet." Then Dad moaned and yanked on his hair again.

While my parents paced round and round like that, I slipped out of the room.

4

Think! Think!

I went out on the back deck and plopped down in the hammock. As I swung back and forth, so did my thoughts. After a while, I felt almost sure of something: The hotel full of my dad's art was OK. The restaurant selling Fish King's seafood was OK. The twelve-plex movie theater for Tess was OK. The stairway from the hotel down to the beach was OK. Even the shops for Dee were OK. But messing with the tide pools was just plain not OK.

Who was it for, anyway? I sat up, put my feet on the ground, and asked myself who on earth would rather have a boring old sandy beach than an interesting rocky one full of hidden life and mystery?

No one, that's who. Or if people did want sandy beaches, there were plenty of them—all up and down the coast! They just don't happen to be here, because sandy beaches don't belong here!

I got up and marched to my room. I went to my bookcase and pulled out my *Guide to Sea Life of Southern California*. I've drawn a little red heart next to the picture and description of every sea creature I've seen with my own eyes. I'm proud of all those hearts. I've been keeping track since I first started snorkeling.

I stuck the book in my pocket and went into the living room to round up my parents. They'd been circling so long that they both looked dizzy.

"Don't you think the best place to figure this out would be at the cove?" I asked them.

They agreed, they grabbed their keys and wallets, and we jumped into the car. But when we got to the beach, we were surprised to see that right where we usually park, there stood ANOTHER sign, exactly like the one on the beach.

We had to park in front of Fish King. One of the Hong brothers waved to us from inside. Their store was as crowded and busy as ever.

We crossed the street and stared at the new sign. This time I noticed the part that said 'Phase One.'

"If this is phase one," I said, "what's phase two?"

"I'm afraid to guess," Dad said with a shiver.

Mom's forehead worried up. "Hmm," she said. "You're right. Where there's a phase one, there has got to be a phase two. Maybe they plan to build the Commercial Cove Resort Amusement Park, with noisy rides, carnival music, and 'Step right up, folks!'"

"Why stop there?" Dad asked. "How about phase three? Commercial Cove Airport! Planes overhead at all hours. Exhaust fumes."

I pulled my parents away from the sign and over to the edge of the cliff. We looked down at white-crested waves and the hazy blue horizon. The beach was Sunday crowded, but I didn't mind. I watched a surfer catch a fantastic ride, and my heart beat faster, imagining what it would be like to be him.

"I think one hospital visit a week is plenty," Dad said. Mom and I agreed. We all climbed extra carefully down the cliff. As soon as we reached the beach, I felt better. The sound of the surf filled my head. The ocean breeze tickled my skin and whipped my hair around. My toes were happy to be wiggling in the warm sand. It was low tide, so the beach was huge, and the rocks showed way, way out there.

Poor Tess, I thought. *How can she stand to be away from this?* I scooped up a handful of sand and put it in my pocket to take to her.

I pulled on my water socks so my feet wouldn't get cut up. Then I crept out along the rocks. All kinds of people were out there: kids, teenagers, grown-ups. All looking into the tide pools and calling to each other, "Hey! Come here! Look at this!"

I went way out where I could be by myself. Then I crouched down and whispered, "Hi, everybody," to the barnacles and sea anemones. My voice was whisked away on the wind and lost in the sound of the crashing waves. A blue crab disappeared into a crack that looked way too small for him. I wondered, for the hundredth time, *How does he do that?*

I watched a nearly see-through fish dart around in its tiny pool. Then I saw a tiny red octopus creep out from between two rocks. I'd never seen one like him before—he was adorable! I leaned close to the rock to say, "Listen up, guys. I'm here to promise you that I won't let your home be taken away. OK?"

No one answered, of course. They didn't seem to be listening, but still, I knew I'd promised, and a promise is a promise, whether anyone hears it or not.

I sat carefully on the seaweed-slippery rocks and pulled out my pen and my book. It took me a pretty long time to find the listing for the tiny red octopus. But then it turned out its name was—duh—"red octopus"! That made me laugh. Its scientific name was *Octopus rubescens.* I drew a heart next to its picture. Then I just sat there, trying to come up with a plan.

Think, think, think! I told myself.

A bit later I saw two people coming straight across the rocks toward me. It took me a while to realize they were my parents. They don't usually came out this far. When they got to me, I showed them the tiny red octopus. Mom knew it was an *Octopus rubescens* right away. She didn't need a sea life guide to tell her it was a baby and to be careful—they bite!

Mom's work is so dry that I sometimes forget it has anything at all to do with the REAL ocean. I mean, I know she's a marine biologist, but it seems like the

ocean she researches is a different one than the one I snorkel, swim, and boogie board in. It's like Mom's ocean is an *idea* of an ocean, a computer screen covered with graphs and charts and rows of numbers—not an actual rock-and-rolly wet place knocked around by the tides.

Her ocean doesn't seem to wiggle with bright turquoise jellyfish or have splashing dolphins, killer whales, or sunken ships.

Dad sat down facing land. Mom and I faced out to sea.

"Look!" Mom pointed.

I followed her finger out to a jutting rock island surrounded by crashing waves. Up on the rock, waving his head back and forth as if he were singing, was a big fat sea lion. We couldn't hear him over the sound of the waves, but we could tell that he was barking at the top of his lungs.

Mom laughed. Then Dad looked toward shore and yelled over the roar of surf and wind, "Remind me that graffiti is illegal."

"Why?" I asked.

"Because," Dad said, "I've half a mind to go over to that stupid Commercial Cove sign and paint these rocks back in where they belong. I'd say, 'Oops, fellas! You forgot to put the tide pools in this picture, but, hey, don't worry about it. I'll fix it right up!' Then I'd whip out my paints and slip, slap–" Dad pantomimed painting gestures in the air—*"Voilà!* All better!"

We got up and picked our way carefully back to the beach. I thought about what Dad had said, and then, BINGO! I knew what to do!

I jumped around on the sand and yelled, "I've got it! We'll have a Commercial Cove Art Protest! All we have to do is hand out a zillion pieces of paper and a bunch of pencils or crayons to everyone who comes to the beach. We'll ask them to draw what they like best about the cove, and . . . well, get it?"

My parents did not look like they got it at all.

I tried again. "Everyone will draw the rocks and that means the tide pools, and we'll get all the pictures together and . . . don't you see?" I held up my sea life book and thumped it. "It's your graffiti idea, Dad. We'll show them that everyone here loves the rocks!"

"Slow down, Kailey. We'll show whom?" Mom asked.

"Whoever is building the resort thing! Whoever is planning to cart away the rocks!"

"Hmm," Dad said, stroking his chin.

"Hmm," agreed Mom.

"Anyway," I added, "we have to try. I promised!"

"Promised whom?" Mom asked.

But instead of answering, I said, "Please? Please, please, PLEASE can we try? All we need is paper and pencils. You wouldn't have to do hardly anything, except drive me to the beach, which you do already."

Mom shrugged. "We couldn't stop the development, but maybe there's hope for the tide pools," she said.

"It's worth a try," Dad agreed.

Hurray! I jumped around shrieking some more until I remembered Tess's broken foot and decided to be a little more careful, at least for now!

By the time I'd calmed down and caught my breath, my parents were sitting close together on a rock, digging their toes into the warm sand and talking. I plopped down next to them and heard Dad say, "Maybe The Man would be interested in seeing Kailey's protest art."

Mom said, "Who?"

"The eighty-eight-painting, two-mural, enough-money-to-live-forever Man," Dad explained. "He likes art. And he's going to need something to hang on all those walls in all those rooms."

I looked up. Dad had that hair-pulling, living-room-pacing look in his eyes again. "You mean you've decided to say no to the commission?" I asked.

Dad sighed. "I'm afraid I have to," he said. "I guess it's the curse of having a conscience."

"But if my protest works, and the tide pools stay, you'll do the paintings, right?"

"Well, right." Dad raked his fingers through his hair again.

"Then cheer up! There's nothing to worry about!" I said.

• • •

Tess was in a lousy mood when I got to her house, but who could blame her? She'd been lying like a lump in that stuffy bedroom for days!

"Can't you use crutches or something?" I asked.

"I tried," Tess said, "but they killed my armpits."

"So you're just going to sit here?" I asked.

"What else am I supposed to do?" Tess asked. "And anyway, it's not like I've got anywhere to go, lugging my cast. All I can do is SIT! How pathetic is that?"

"Well, you could sit in different places," I said.

Tess rolled her eyes. "Give me a break."

So I tried to change the subject. "I brought you something," I said, opening my fist to show her my handful of sand.

"Watch it!" she snapped. "You're getting it in my bed! And why'd you bring that here, anyway? Just to rub it in that YOU get to go to the beach and I don't? That you can have a normal summer and I can't? Gee, thanks, Kailey, you're the ultimate pal."

I closed my fist and put it back in my pocket. "Sorry," I said, backing away from her. I'd never seen Tess so cranky. I knew she probably couldn't help it, but still, I had to make myself stay in the room because what I really wanted to do was run.

I didn't dare sit on even the tip-edge of her bed, so I sat on the floor and said, "I got an idea today, about the tide pools."

"What about them?" Tess asked in a bored voice.

"You know, about how to save them."

Tess rolled her eyes for the tenth time. "Are you still on THAT?"

"Yeah," I choked. "I am." I tried to keep my voice normal, but Tess was being so mean that I didn't know what to say to her.

"OK," she sighed. "Tell me your brilliant idea."

I practically felt tears come into my eyes. "I never said it was brilliant," I said. "It's just an idea."

"Whatever," Tess sighed again. "Like I care."

Then she picked up the remote and hit power.

Loud TV voices suddenly filled the room. I got up and moved toward the door.

"Well, bye," I said. "I'll see you tomorrow or something. OK?" But Tess didn't even bother to wave.

• • •

I found my parents with Lynn in the kitchen. They all looked surprised to see me back so soon.

"Is Tess asleep?" Lynn asked me.

"No."

"Does she need something? A glass of milk?" Lynn asked. "Help getting to the bathroom?"

I shrugged my shoulders. "I don't think so," I said, feeling like a miserable failure.

Finally Mom (my hero) figured out that something wasn't right and got to her feet. "Sorry for such a short visit, Lynn, but we've gotta run," she said.

Dad got the hint and stood up, too.

As she walked us to the door, Lynn said, "I'm so glad you came by, Kailey. Tess has been a little depressed."

That made me feel really guilty for being such a crummy friend. Not only hadn't I cheered Tess up, but I seemed to have made her even gloomier than she was before.

On the way to the car, Dad asked me what Tess thought of my cove-art, save-the–tide-pools idea. When I said, "I didn't tell her," Mom and Dad exchanged looks.

Ick. I felt awful. And hadn't I felt great just a tiny while ago? I hunched down in the backseat of the car and let my thoughts bash around in my head like a kayak in a typhoon. When did everything get so confusing? I know when. It was when that SIGN came along!

I wished I'd never seen it. I wished I could just be happy about the "moo-vies" like Tess. I wished I didn't care about the tide pools. I wished someone else was taking care of the tide-pool creatures so I could forget about them!

I wished I could get into the water and let the tide

wash all these thoughts away. I wanted to forget Tess and her bad mood and broken foot. Forget the tide pools and Dad's painting commission and my art idea.

I closed my eyes and imagined myself in snorkel mask and fins, floating weightlessly on my belly. Schools of pretty blue fish darted and turned below me. Spongy pink anemones wiggled their tentacles, and I pictured kelp swaying gracefully in the tide. Everything down there was crystal clear and peaceful. *Ahhhh.*

But then it occurred to me that if I wanted to keep my lovely beach, I couldn't let the Commercial Cove people ruin it. My eyes popped open.

The sign had said "Coming Soon," so there was no time to lose. I had to get my hands on some paper and pencils and start handing them out. How was I going to do all that? And how soon was "Soon"?

At dinner, my parents and I talked about the Commercial Cove Art Protest. They said they supported me one hundred percent, but they also told me not to get my hopes up. "A lot of adults in town have been trying to stop this resort," Dad said. "Petitions, lawyers . . . We just want you to know that we think your plan is worth a try, as long as you understand that it might not work."

"Oh, it'll work," I told him. "It has to!"

Right before bed, Dad presented me with a package of computer paper and a box of pencils. Wow, I was really, really going to do this! I wished Tess could help me. It would be way more fun if we could do this together. That is, if she got over being so grumpy.

5

Bummer, Dude

We got to the bluff early, just as the dawn surfers were leaving. It was cold and foggy. Looking down at the cove, I could barely make out the smudgy white break of the waves. The sea was glassy under the haze, and there was no horizon at all.

Dad nudged me, bringing my mind back to earth.

"Oh yeah!" I said. "Right!"

I ran up to a surfer who had his wet suit half peeled down. He was carrying a really gorgeous board. "Excuse me," I said. "I'm trying to get, I mean, we all have to—no, wait. This is about the resort thingie project? With the movies and everything? You know, the tide pools?"

The surfer looked down at me and said, "Whatever, kid. I've gotta get to work." And he walked off.

Two other surfers were heading off in different directions. I chased after one, calling, "Excuse me! Excuse me!" But she didn't hear me and just kept walking.

This was NOT going well.

I looked over at Dad. He smiled sympathetically.

I practically tackled the next surfer as soon as he reached the top of the cliff. "I'm trying to get people to draw pictures of the cove," I gushed. "And I'm going to give them to the resort builder developer guys to make them not want to destroy the tide pools." That wasn't exactly brilliant, but at least the guy was still there and listening. "So," I went on, "it's sort of an art protest. Will you draw one?"

I ripped open the package of paper and pulled out a sheet. Actually I accidentally pulled out a bunch of sheets and when I tried to shove them back in, some of them wrinkled and crunched and some got

away from me altogether and blew out across the
bluff. Dad chased the runaways for me while I fished
around in my pocket for a pencil to hand the surfer.
But by then he had wandered away. I chased after
him, yelling, "Wait! Will you do a drawing?"

He turned back to me and said something that I
didn't understand. Dad said later that he thought it
was in Hungarian.

Meanwhile, other surfers had escaped. I did catch
the last one, who said,
"Cool, but I'm all, like,
wet? And my hands
are, like, frozen? Like,
holding a pencil
would be, like, totally
impossible? Sorry,
dude. Later."

Dude? Dad and I
laughed. Dude in a
sundress?

We went across the bluff to the diner. The painting on the diner wall was by my dad. It was the view from the diner's big bay window. You could look out the window, and then look at the painting of the scene out the same window. It was like seeing someone in two different moods, the same face wearing two different expressions. I love that.

We got the bay-window table, and I compared the two views. There's a clear blue sky in Dad's painting, with a few small clouds either coming or going off to the side. The real view out the window today was still foggy and gray, but the fog would probably clear and the day could turn out just like Dad's painting. It was like looking into the future.

I asked Julia, the waitress, if she'd draw a picture of the cove for my protest.

"Me? I haven't drawn in years!" she said, batting away the piece of paper I held out to her. "And in front of your daddy? Get him to draw your protest! He's the artist around here."

"It's not about how good an artist you are," I said. "It's just a drawing, not, like, a *drawing!*"

Julia shook her head no. Then she whipped out her order pad, pulled the pen out from behind her ear, and said, "What'll it be?"

Dad ordered coffee and a scone. I ordered raisin toast and hot cocoa.

I watched Julia's thin gray braid sway down her back as she headed around the counter to the kitchen. She once told me that she had never had a haircut, ever. And for Julia, "ever" is a long time.

When she came back with Dad's coffee, Julia said, "I think it's mighty fine that you're trying to do something to stop all that destruction over there. My daughter and her family think it'll be the bee's knees having the resort mess here—but I don't."

"Then draw for me!" I begged.

But she said, "Nope. Sorry. Can't."

Then a family with a bunch of kids came in and sat at a table by the door. Dad gave me a hopeful thumbs-up and said, "You go, girl!"

So I marched over to their table and tried my very, very best to explain my project to them. They seemed to understand me and said they were willing to do some drawings.

I gave them paper and pencils, thinking, *All right! My first success!*

Then the mom looked up at me and said, "You don't have to stand there. We'll leave them for you on the table when we're done."

"Oh, OK, great!" I stammered, embarrassed for hanging around them when they didn't want me to. Then I practically ran back to my table.

Julia placed their order and then brought Dad and me our food. But it doesn't take long to eat scones and raisin toast. So once we'd eaten every crumb, we had to just sit there twirling our thumbs, waiting for the family of drawers to finish eating. They'd ordered a huge breakfast—omelets, waffles, sausage, hash browns, orange juice, muffins, tea . . .

When at last they threw their napkins on their plates and pushed themselves away from the table, I jumped to my feet. But then the father put on his glasses and started s-l-o-w-l-y checking over the bill, so I sat back down.

I thought they'd never leave. When they finally did, I zoomed over to their table and GROSS! One "drawing" had maple syrup and a glob of gooey egg spilled on it. Another was sort of a beach, I guess, but it was full of army tanks and crashing warplanes and flaming helicopters! One (probably the baby's) was just scribbling. Another "drawing" was a shopping list—paper towels, cleanser, apples, eggs. One of the parents must've done that. And all the pencils were gone!

I dragged myself back to our table and collapsed in my chair.

"Bummer, dude," Dad said.

• • •

OK, so this wasn't going exactly right. In fact, I

couldn't imagine how it could go much worse. Suddenly, all I really, really wanted to do was forget the whole stupid thing and go for a swim. But Dad pointed out the window at the flower shop/nursery where Jeremy, the owner, was turning his sign around from *Cerado,* which is the Spanish word for "closed," to *Abierto,* which means "open."

"Ready?" Dad asked me. I wasn't, but we said good-bye to Julia and left.

The haze had mostly melted and I could feel the sun as we crossed to Jeremy's shop. Bells jingled when we opened his door. It smelled great in there. I took a deep breath. Ah! My second-favorite smell!

Jeremy was singing along with the opera on the radio while he watered. He held up one finger, telling us to wait until the end of the music. We did.

Jeremy's voice and his gestures got bigger and bigger until the end. Then he snapped off the radio and bowed, getting water all over the floor. Dad and I applauded and cheered. "Bravo! Bravo!"

I love Jeremy. He always gives me a flower when we visit him. This time he handed me a beautiful purple iris.

I thanked him but gave it right back. "I'm here on business and I need both my hands," I said. Jeremy listened to my whole long explanation of the Commercial Cove Art Protest and said he thought it sounded "marvelous."

Jeremy carefully dried his hands and took a piece of paper from me. He said I should return at the end of the day for his masterpiece. Then he said he'd tell everyone who walked into his shop about my plan and he'd simply insist that they put pencil to paper.

I thanked him a million times and left a stack of paper on his desk for his customers to use. Then Dad and I left, making the bells chime again.

It was sunnier out now and I could practically HEAR the water calling to me. "Kailey," it said, "grab your board and come on in!"

And boy, did I want to! But instead, Dad and I

went from store to store and stopped people on the street. Most people were nice, but not everyone. Some pretended that I was invisible. Some practically ran from me. It took all my strength to keep from making ugly faces at them behind their backs.

Then there were those people who wouldn't look at me or listen to me, but who held out quarters and dimes as if I were spare-changing. They were always surprised that I wouldn't take the money.

A few people told me they thought I was crazy. "The resort is the first good thing to come to this town," one man said. "I personally hope it's just the beginning!"

"I'm not against the resort!" I called after him. "Just the wrecking of the beach! The tide pools!" But he was gone.

"Don't meddle in things you're too young to understand," one woman snapped.

Another one threatened to call the police on me for harassment! Then she spotted my dad and shook her finger at him, saying, "Shame on you! Sending a child out to do your dirty work!"

Some families let their kids do drawings for me, but the grown-ups just stood there. Or they told me they couldn't draw a straight line, as if straight lines had anything to do with it! I wanted drawings done by EVERYONE, not just kids, because I was afraid that the adult building developer people wouldn't take kids' drawings very seriously. I know I've been told that kids can make a difference in the world, but I wondered if that was really true.

When Dad told me it was only eleven o'clock in the morning, I thought he was kidding. It felt like at least dinnertime!

"It's going pretty well," he said. "You should feel proud."

"You've got to be kidding," I said. But he wasn't.

An hour later, when we finally, finally stopped back at the diner for lunch, I was totally beat and my feet hurt. I barely had the strength to chew my grilled cheese sandwich. And all I had to show for it was a handful of wrinkled drawings, none of them very impressive. I showed them to Julia when she brought the bill.

"Well, they're a sight better than I could've done," she said. "I told you that my son-in-law is the big cheese over at the cove project, didn't I?"

Huh? We shook our heads no and I said, "Why didn't you say so before?"

"Well, it embarrasses me," she said. "But for better or for worse, he's the fellow who came to town way back when they first started sniffing around the cove. Five years ago? Six? Yep, he took one look at my Connie and that was that. Wedding bells."

I thought that sounded kind of romantic.

Julia went on. "I've told him we don't want his old resort here, but he doesn't listen to me. Now he's got my daughter and my grandbabies thinking the resort's going to be the greatest thing on earth. Their own personal kingdom! They'll live like royalty."

Dad and I listened with our mouths hanging open.

"They already live too high off the hog, if you ask me. More money than is decent. Those babies, I love them dearly, but they're just plain spoiled. Spoiled rotten!" Julia sighed. "Luther, that's my son-in-law, tried to get me to retire. Said he'd pay all my expenses so I could sit on my ever-expanding butt and watch soaps all day, growing old. So I said to him, I said, 'No thanks! That's not living; that's waiting to die.' So he said I could wait tables over to the resort when it's built, make big tips. And I said, 'I'm happy where I am, thank you very much.' Can you picture me slinging hash in a snazzy joint like that?"

"Did you say Luther?" Dad asked.

"Luther Drake, resident hotshot," Julia said.

Dad's eyes grew round. "That's the guy who called me," he said. "Luther Drake is The Man about the art."

Julia didn't look a bit surprised. "He loves that

picture," she said, pointing at Dad's painting of the view out the diner's bay window. "Always has, since the first time he walked in here. Asked me, in fact, if he and my Connie could have it as a wedding gift!"

"No kidding?" Dad asked.

"No kidding," Julia answered. Then the cook dinged his bell, and she ran back to pick up an order.

"That's SOOOO perfect!" I said.

"What is?" Dad asked.

"Well, now we know who to show the tide-pool drawings to!"

"Who?"

"Da-ad, don't play dumb! Julia's son-in-law, of course! When you go to see him about your painting commission, I'll come along and I'll bring all the amazing pictures I'll have collected by then. And," I took a deep breath, "we'll explain to him that the rocks have to stay, and you'll tell him you're going to paint the rocks where they belong, and he'll see that it makes much more sense to just let nature design its own beaches. And in case he doesn't get it, you can tell him you'll paint the cove WITH the tide pools on his lobby wall, or you won't paint it at all. So there!"

Then I asked my dad why he was looking at me like that.

"Because," Dad said, imitating my tone, "Mr. Drake will say, 'Well, thanks anyway, Pete, but there are plenty of fish in the sea. Or, in this case, artists in the town.'"

"No, he won't!" I insisted. "We'll show him a whole huge heap of beach drawings done by everyone who comes here. Then you can tell him that your painting will be based on what the people drew. Get it?"

Dad smiled his biggest smile and said, "You must've gotten your courage from Mom's side of the family."

After lunch we climbed down the cliff. "There's not enough gas in the car for a trip to the emergency room today," Dad said out of habit, but he didn't have to. Since Tess's accident I'd been very, very careful.

It was Monday, so the beach was nearly empty. I tried to get the few people there to do drawings for me but had no luck. They were mostly interested in being left alone. Plus, it was really windy and the only thing my papers wanted to do was fly away.

One man asked me if this was a school project.

I said, "No, it's summer."

And he blew up at me! "You don't have to tell me it's summer, young lady," he practically yelled. "I was a principal for thirty-two years! I know more about summer than you ever will! And let me ask you this: Haven't you heard of year-round school? Or summer school, for that matter?"

Then the principal marched off in disgust, muttering about how rude children are these days. It's hard to march in sand.

Phew! I was super glad he wasn't the principal at *my* school.

I don't know how much of the principal's rant my dad heard, but I guess he heard enough to take pity on me. Because as soon as the principal was gone, Dad said, "As long as we're here, do you want to go for a quick swim?"

YESSS! Before he even finished his sentence, I shoved my papers into his hands, slipped off my sundress, and charged into the waves. Ah! The roar, crash, hiss of the tide filled my ears at last!

I didn't have my boogie board, so I did some body-whomping, which was a blast. And without a board to keep track of, I could just roll around. As I looked up from under the white water, the bubbles looked like storm clouds. I love that.

When Dad gave me the signal to come in, I wanted to pretend I didn't see him. But I knew that would make him really mad, so I came out of the water and sprawled next to him on the sand.

He said he'd been thinking—maybe we needed to make some changes in the art protest.

"You bet we do," I agreed.

"I think we need a booth or something," he said. "And we need to give something away."

"Like what?" I asked.

"Like I don't know what" was his answer. "But people with causes are always giving freebies— refrigerator magnets, or pencils with 'Save the Whales' printed on them. Even when you vote, you get a little flag sticker that says 'I Voted.'"

Hmm. I'd have to think about that. If we gave away little rocks or shells or something, *we'd* be the ones destroying the tide pools, bit by bit!

Meanwhile, I asked six more people on the beach to do drawings and only one said yes—another little kid. Dad thought one in six was good. I thought it stunk.

I got dressed and we climbed back up the cliff. Before we got into the car to go home, we stopped at Jeremy's shop. When he saw us, he came scurrying up wagging a bunch of papers.

"Not one leaf left the store the entire day," he

announced, "until the customer had delivered a cove sketch. And they're brilliant! Every last one of them. Absolutely brilliant."

Jeremy was right, the pictures were brilliant, and what was brilliant about them was that they ALL had the tide-pool rocks in them. I thanked him and thanked him.

"No problem, lovey," he said. "And I'd be honored to have my customers draw for their flora tomorrow as well."

Hurray for Jeremy! And he even remembered to give me that beautiful purple iris when I was leaving!

Dad asked if I wanted to stop at Tess's house on the way home. I was tired, but I said, "Sure," so we did.

The good news: Tess was out on her front porch swing instead of cooped up in her bedroom. The bad news: she was in even a worse mood than yesterday!

I offered to braid her hair in tiny braids, but she said, "What's the point? It's not like I'm going any-where. And even if I did, anyone who saw me would be too busy staring at my cast and my scarred-up face to notice my hair!"

I sat on the steps and said, "I'm sorry you feel so bad." I started picking burrs out of my dress.

After neither of us said anything for a while, Tess said, "I'm just so BORED and MAD and I just HATE this! And it's going to go ON and ON for practically the whole summer!"

I nodded and asked her if she wanted to know what I did today.

First she said, "NO!" but then she sighed and said, "OK, tell me."

So I did. Including the diner family that kept me and Dad waiting forever, and the surfer who called me DUDE.

Tess laughed and finally seemed more like herself. "As long as you're sure you're NOT trying to stop anyone from building the movie theaters or the mall," she said. "It sounds like fun to chase people around and bug them to draw the tide pools."

"Hey!" I said, suddenly excited. "My dad thinks we should have a booth. YOU could be the booth!"

Tess said, "Huh?"

"You know! We could set up a table and chair, and put an umbrella over it or something, so you don't totally fry. And maybe we'd have a big sign saying I don't know what, something about drawing to save the tide pools or whatever. And you'd sit there and—"

"Yes!" Tess said. "I could absolutely do that! And people would come up and I'd give them paper and—"

"I LOVE it!" I cheered. "I totally LOVE it!"

"Me too!" Tess giggled.

"And your crutches will be perfect! When we go with my dad to see the art commission guy, you'll hobble in with our drawings and he'll totally pity the girl in the cast!"

Tess giggled harder.

I stood up to act out Luther. In a low, Santa-like voice I said, "Yes, of course! I will leave the tide pools alone if it makes poor Tess feel better. Ho-ho-ho!"

Tess and I plotted and planned, happy as could be, until Dad came out onto the porch and said it was time to go.

"Oh yeah," I said, pointing at my dad. "He thinks we should give something away."

"You mean like prizes?" she asked.

"Like stickers that say 'I Voted,'" I said.

Tess looked confused, but I didn't stop to explain.

"I'll call you later," I said, and we left.

6

A Done Deal

Mom came home from work loaded with goodies for me. It turned out that the people she works with loved the idea of my art protest, and everyone wanted to help! One scientist gave Mom a box of twenty pencils to give to me. Another one donated three big packages of paper. And Mom's boss told her to tell me that if I needed to use their copy machine or anything, to let him know.

And everyone at Mom's lab did drawings! The best one was done on the computer by Mom's research assistant, Uri. I thought it was pretty enough to frame, and Dad thought so, too.

• • •

Tess and I called each other back and forth so many
times that night that Mom threatened to take away my
phone privileges. But Tess sounded so much happier
now that she had something to plan for and think about
besides her scarred face. Before we hung up the last time,
Tess said, "When I told my sister about your plan, Dee
thought I meant a *drawing* instead of a drawing."

I said, "A what instead of a who?"

"You know, a drawing like when you draw the
winning raffle ticket out of a hat and win a door prize,
that kind of thing?"

"That's brilliant!" I cheered.

"Huh?"

"We could do both—have people do a drawing
AND have them enter a DRAWING. I love it! An art
protest contest!"

In the morning, Dad took me to Tess's house and
we got to work. First we painted a sign, red paint on
white poster board, that said, "DRAW for the TIDE
POOLS."

The paint was a little drippy, so the sign ended up looking kind of scary, like Halloween blood. But that was OK. Tess had an old fishbowl, and we decided to use that for the raffle tickets, if we could make some or find some.

"But what'll we raffle off?" asked Tess.

"Well," I said, thinking, "maybe the prize could be . . . one of my dad's drawings? Do a drawing for a draw for a drawing?"

"Would he do that? Give one away for free?" Tess asked.

"I don't know," I admitted. "I haven't asked." But then I had another idea. "Wait!" I said. "How about raffling off a tour of the tide pools? My mom could take someone out there and tell them all about the plants and the fish and all that."

Tess nodded. "My mom's not a scientist," she said, "but I bet I could get her to bake some of her lemon squares for the winner to eat while they're getting the tide-pool tour."

I said, "Yum!" Lynn's lemon squares are UNbelievably incredible.

"And if Dee's in a good mood, maybe she'll polish the winner's nails," Tess added. "And you could braid their hair! And I could . . . what could I do?"

"We could give them bodyboard lessons!" I said.

"But what if the winner is really old or a baby?" Tess laughed, and I did too.

And we were ready to go to the beach.

When we got there, Dad unloaded the card table and folding chairs. I carried the sign and a roll of tape and the fishbowl, and Tess hobbled out on her crutches.

We set up under a shady tree and taped our bloody sign to the front of the table. Tess sat on her folding chair like a queen on her throne, with her stack of papers, her cup of pencils, and her empty fishbowl.

As we were setting up, we saw Jeremy come out of his store across the street with one pink rose in a tiny vase, to decorate our booth. Wasn't that sweet?

But do you know who came after Jeremy? NO ONE! That is, there were people around, wandering in and out of the stores and standing nearby looking down from the bluff at the view, but no one came over to our booth.

Tess and I each took a piece of paper and started on our own drawings of the cove. I'm not the artist my dad is, but I'm not bad, and Tess is pretty good, too. She does extremely careful, slow work, drawing each rock with tiny microscopic details.

I draw with big long lines, sort of zip-zap-dash. But today, I couldn't even sit still long enough to do that. My foot was drumming until Tess told me to cut it out. "You're shaking the whole table!" she complained. I tried to relax and concentrate on drawing, but I couldn't. So I got up, grabbed paper and pencils, and started running after people again.

One woman got offended. "Don't you remember me, dear? I did a drawing for you yesterday!" she said.

"Oh yeah!" I said, feeling awful. "Of course!" Although the truth was I didn't remember her at all.

I crept back to Tess at the booth. "Convincing that Luther guy not to destroy the tide pools will be a cinch compared to trying to get people to draw pictures!"

Meanwhile, Tess was folding and ripping paper into little squares to be our raffle tickets—in case we ever got someone to give them to. She said, "We should make a sign or something that says, 'Super duper amazing prizes to be announced later!' or—" Tess giggled—"'Surprise prizes'!"

"Maybe we could list all the things the prizes MIGHT be," I said, "like maybe a free trip to Hawaii! Maybe a tour of the tide pools! Enter and find out!"

Then an older teenage guy looked like he was actually walking toward our booth. Tess and I got so excited, we grabbed hands under the table and tried not to squeak. Our first booth customer!

When he got close enough, he read our sign out loud. "Draw for the tide pools?" he said. "Wow! You mean, if I win I get to keep them?"

Tess started to giggle.

I said, "I beg your pardon?"

"Keep the tide pools?" he asked. "Will someone, like, deliver them to my place?" He didn't seem to be kidding.

Tess giggled more. I wanted to giggle, but the guy was practically a grown-up and I didn't dare laugh at him. I tried to explain our project instead.

He listened and nodded, but at the end, when I said, "Would you like to do a drawing?" he said, "Naaah, no thanks."

Tess practically fell off her chair laughing, but I managed to keep my straight face till he'd wandered away.

After a while some kids from school rode up. Mandy was on a mountain bike, Chloe rode her scooter, Destiny was on Rollerblades, and her little brother, whose name I don't know, was trying to skateboard. His grinds were pathetic.

Tess and I were THRILLED to see familiar, friendly faces. "You look like a TV commercial!" I called out to them. "Like a toothpaste ad, or an ad for pizza."

Tess agreed.

"I've always wanted to be in a commercial," Destiny yelled back, striking a pose on her blades.

Then they all circled our table. We told them about our Commercial Cove Art Protest.

"I want to help," Chloe said.

"I just HATE the idea of some bully messing with our cove!" Mandy agreed, looking like she'd knock the head off anyone who tried. Then they each took some paper and headed off in different directions.

When we were alone again, Tess said, "That's the idea! Get people to do all our work for us!"

But I couldn't bear to just sit there another second. I was itching to get moving. "OK," I told Tess, "the booth is all yours. I'm off!"

"But I thought we were going to sit here together!" Tess whined.

"If we're going to make adult developers change their grown-up minds about their big grown-up adult plans, we need buckets and tons of drawings. Heaps and truckloads full," I told her. "We have to make the developers' eyes bug out! It has to shock, daze, and amaze them. Knock their socks off!"

"All right, all right," Tess said. "So go already."

My dad had set up his easel not too far away. He looked over at us and gave us the thumbs-up.

I climbed down the cliff, clutching a hunk of paper, with a bunch of pencils jammed into my back pocket. I was determined to REALLY get some drawings this time. No more Miss Nice Girl.

I barreled up to a family who were having a picnic. Their radio was full-blast KROQ. They didn't hear me coming, but their dog did. He ran up to me with a green tennis ball in his mouth, ready to play. The rest of the family wasn't as friendly at first.

But when I explained what I was doing, they all wanted to help. The mom said she thought it was outrageous that anyone would even think of carting away our rocks!

I handed them each a pencil and some paper, and I played with their yellow Lab while they drew. What a sweetie!

Then, with their drawings safely in my hand, I marched over to a surfer who was waxing his board, and I did my talk again. He said he wasn't from around here, but I said it didn't matter. "The beach belongs to everyone who uses it," I said.

"Cool," he said. And he drew me a really gnarly drawing. He was totally surfer but he didn't call me "dude."

After him, I ran up to a beachcomber and got her to put down her basket of driftwood and shells and do a quick drawing. It was my lucky day. Ding! Ding! Ding! The drawings were adding up. By the time I climbed back up to Tess and my dad, I had nine. Not exactly truckloads. It wasn't going to make any developer's eyes bug out, but I told myself that it wasn't half bad for only ten o'clock in the morning!

I figured I could stay down on the beach longer and wait for more people, maybe even sneak in a little swim or a quick visit to the tide pools while I was there. But then I thought of poor, broken-footed Tess stuck at our booth alone, probably bored out of her mind. So I made myself climb back up.

I found Tess excited and full of smiles. She said that while I'd been down at the beach, a camp bus had parked near her and emptied out oodles of campers who were here to go on the firehouse tour. Tess said she grabbed her crutches and waved them in the air to get the attention of the teenage camp counselors. When they came over to her, Tess begged them to do tide-pool drawings, and by some miracle, they agreed!

They had camp crayons and everything in their bus, so we didn't even have to supply the paper. And all ninety zillion kids sat down near our booth and drew what they saw. Tess told me that even the bus driver and counselors did tide-pool drawings. The stack was really high!

I danced around the booth cheering, and Tess thumped the table with her crutches, making the pencils jump. We told Dad that our good luck meant we'd earned a break at the diner. I was craving French toast.

Someone already had the bay-window table, so we sat at the counter. I didn't spin on my stool because Tess couldn't. Dad dragged a chair over for Tess's cast.

After we ordered, I went around to the other breakfast-eaters and asked them to do drawings. Some said no, some said yes. Thinking of the family yesterday, I wanted to ask the yes people not to slobber on their artwork, but I didn't.

As we were leaving, Destiny and her brother flew

through the door, practically knocking Tess off her crutches. They were sweaty and out of breath but smiling from ear to ear.

"You won't believe this!" Destiny chirped, handing me a batch of drawings. "These are by the mechanics at Boris's Auto and some of the people who were waiting around for their cars to get fixed. AND these are from all the people at Millie's Donuts!"

This batch was great news. Our stack was getting serious now. REALLY serious!

Tess was moving pretty slowly on those crutches so it took us a while to get back across the road to our booth. But as soon as we did, Mandy rode up on her bike and gave us some drawings by her family and her neighbor.

"Fantabulous!" Tess said.

No one knew where Chloe was, but Mandy bet she'd gone to her mom's hair salon. Probably she was getting all the people there to draw for her. Between the hair stylists and shampooers and manicurists and

customers, that would be a lot of drawings!
I wondered if Chloe's pictures would stink of
hair stuff.

While we were all standing around our table
(except Tess, who was sitting), one of the firemen
showed up and said he'd heard about us from the
campers who were at the station on tour. He said
that unless there was an emergency today, we
could stop by later and the firefighters would
make drawings. *Cool. That'd be way fun.*

Suddenly everything seemed to be going great.
Destiny and Mandy gave each other high fives and
congratulated themselves on how well they'd done.

"Piece of cake!" said Destiny.

"The tide pools are as good as saved," Mandy
agreed.

Chloe scootered up with a backpack full of
drawings. She took them out and held them up
like a teacher reading a picture book to the class.
"This one is by Harriet Goldbaum," Chloe said.

"Tanya was giving her a perm and tint." Chloe held up the next one. "Evelyn Bernstein-Silk, pedicure by Gabby. Mrs. Hill, cut and color by Marcus."

By the time Chloe was done introducing each drawing by its artist and the beauty treatment at her mom's shop, we were all laughing too hard to breathe. When everyone recovered, each girl took fresh paper and headed off to collect more drawings.

Then a man came up to our booth, and Tess and I launched into our "save the tide pools" speech. We'd gotten pretty good at it, compared to my bumbling and fumbling in the beginning. The man listened, but then he shook his head and said, "I just heard about your protest from the florist." He pointed back over his shoulder toward Jeremy's store. "That's why I came over here. I thought someone should tell you girls that you're wasting your time."

"Well, it's worth a try," I said. "So would you like to do a drawing and enter our drawing drawing?"

This still cracked Tess up.

"You don't get it," he said. "I mean, it's seriously a waste of time. I have it on good authority that the marina scheme is a done deal."

Huh? I must have looked blank. "Marina scheme? What marina scheme?"

Tess stopped laughing.

"I'm sorry to disappoint you," he said.

Tess and I looked at each other, thinking: *A marina? Boats? Docks? Water traffic? That would mean no swimming, no boogie boarding. Toxic diesel swirls in the water.* We wrinkled up our noses and both said, "EEEW!"

"Are you sure about this?" I asked the man.

He nodded and said, "My neighbor is one of the big honchos on this marina plan. He's been talking about it for months, and it sure sounds to me like it's a done deal. So, like I said, you're wasting your time."

I don't know what Tess was doing, but I know I was staring at that man with my mouth hanging open in shock. Finally he said, "I just thought you'd want to know." Then he shrugged and walked away.

"Tess! Can that be right? Do you think that guy knows what he's talking about?"

"Nah," Tess said. "He's GOT to be making it up. Doesn't he?"

"I don't know," I said. "There's no marina on the sign. Why would it be such a secret?"

"Beats me," Tess said.

I looked at Dad, painting calmly at his easel. We called him over and told him what the guy had said.

"There it is," Dad sighed. "That's what we've been waiting for."

"There what is?" I asked.

"WHAT were we waiting for?" Tess asked.

"Phase two, of course," Dad said, and the way he said it gave me goosebumps.

7

Lemon Squares

"A marina is a very big deal," Dad said. "They don't just want a pretty beach; they must want a money-making beach. Dock rentals, boat rentals, maybe mechanics and a filling station—"

"It's hopeless, then," I said, looking at the drawings we'd collected.

After a second, Tess perked up. "You think they'll rent sailboards and water skis and water bikes and stuff like that?"

Dad nodded. "Possibly."

"Well, that'll be fun!" Tess said. Then she looked at me, and I guess the look on my face reminded her of the tide-pool animals or of boogie boarding or of snorkeling or all of that put together. She stopped smiling and said, "Oh, right, I forgot."

• • •

We'd just packed up our booth and our drawings and were dragging ourselves sadly to the car when Jeremy came running over. "Why are you leaving so early?" he asked.

"I thought you knew," I said. "That man said he heard about us from you."

"Yes, and it's simply wretched, and he was an awful man," Jeremy said. "And he didn't buy so much as a bud. But I still do not understand why you're packing up so early."

I blinked at him. Hadn't he understood?

"It's all over," Tess explained. "It turns out they're hauling away the tide pools so they can put in a marina."

"We thought they were just destroying the tide pools for the heck of it," I added. "Just because they thought an empty beach would look better, or because they didn't want to get blamed if resort guests fell on the rocks or something. But it's much, much bigger than we thought."

Jeremy shuddered, "I know, it's ghastly. But doesn't that make you even madder?"

"Sure it does!" I said.

"Then why are you giving up?" he asked. "Don't just run off. Let's have some pie and discuss this, shall we?"

I shrugged. Jeremy ushered us all into the diner, holding the door for Tess and her clunky crutches.

We sat around the bay-window table feeling gloomy.

"How you folks doing?" Julia asked.

"Julia, did you know that they were planning to build a MARINA in the cove?" I asked.

"Of course, honey. We talked about this, don't you remember?"

"No," I said, "I don't. I thought they were just taking away the rocks so tourists wouldn't trip on them."

"A parking lot for boats, I'm telling you," Julia said. "And a crying shame it is, too."

Some people came into the diner, and I automatically got up to go beg them for drawings, but then I sat right back down without doing it.

"It seems silly to quit now, though," Jeremy said, "when you've already collected so many excellent drawings."

"He has a point," Dad agreed.

"We did promise people that we'd use their drawings as a protest," Tess said. "We'd kind of be lying if we didn't still SHOW them to someone. Right?" she said, looking at me.

"Quit? You're thinking of giving it up?" Julia asked.

I shrugged. Everyone was looking at me.

Julia dealt out menus and went to ring up a woman who was leaving.

"I don't know," I said. "A marina is a whole different thing. And if Julia's son-in-law doesn't give a hoot about her opinion of the resort, why would he care about our opinion of the marina?"

"Trust me," Jeremy said, rolling his eyes, "NO ONE

cares about his mother-in-law's opinions."

"Well, none of the petitions and community meetings mattered either," I said. I looked around at the sad faces at the table and wished I was lying belly-down on my board, catching a wave, and riding without a thought in my head besides "Wheeeee!"

Tess said, "Well, it's probably hopeless, but it always was!"

Everyone groaned.

"No, seriously," she went on. "Why should the marina make any difference?"

Then Dad started nodding. "Tess is right, actually. "Either way you're fighting a giant."

"The stakes are certainly higher now than any of us suspected," Jeremy agreed, "and therefore worth MORE effort, not less."

Julia showed up with waters for everyone. Then she fished around in her deep apron pocket and pulled out a piece of paper, which she waved in my face. "You won't be needing this, then, right?"

"You drew a picture for us?" I asked.

"I did. Last night. And it came out a sight better than I expected, I'll tell you that!" Julia said proudly.

Tess lunged for it. "Let me see! Let me see!"

Dad and Jeremy were tipping forward too, out of curiosity.

Julia waggled her picture out of my reach.

"OK, then," I said. "I guess I'm still game if all of you are."

Everyone cheered, and Julia handed me her drawing. It was incredible! She'd divided the paper into four squares and each one was a different panel, like in a cartoon strip. The first one showed our cove, rocks and all.

The second had the cove full of white docks like long teeth in an evil grin. The masts of a million boats stabbed up into the sky like spears. No rocks were to be seen.

The third panel was her grandest drawing, show-ing the scene gone wild, with huge tsunami waves, a killer whale ramming into the docks, boats crashing, people leaping overboard into the open mouths of sharks! It also had fish leaping out of the water to smack sailors with their tails, and crabs pinching sailors' butts with their claws!

The fourth panel showed the cove in a mess. Planks of wood were strewn on the shore. Smashed, capsized boats lay in a sea of litter. Sailors were pinned under a beached shark with X's for eyes. Crabs and fish and whales congratulated each other. A revenge of the sea!

"Haven't doodled in probably thirty years, so I'm a bit rusty," Julia said, blushing. "Just wanted to do my part to help out."

We all gaped at Julia.

She whipped out her order pad and said, "What'll it be, folks? Soup today is navy bean."

• • •

When Mom came home and found Dad and me crashed on the couch, she collapsed with us.

I'd never been so tired in my entire life. Neither Dad nor I had the strength to tell Mom about our day, so for a while we all just sprawled in a mess of tired arms and legs. But eventually we told her about the marina.

Then Mom told us that some of her coworkers at the lab had actually been doing a study on the effect of heavy boat traffic on the marine environment.

"What do you mean?" I asked.

"They've been researching how marinas impact the plants and animals. Exactly like the situation would be in our cove," she said. "Some of these are the same people who did those drawings for you yesterday."

I dragged myself off the sofa and showed her the cove cartoon strip by Julia.

Mom thought it was great, but she pointed out, "Unfortunately, that's *not* how it will be. Once they've cleared away the rocks and the kelp and have filled the area with fuel exhaust and litter, the water will be pretty dead."

"No revenge of the sea? No butt-pinching crabs?" I asked.

"No," Mom said. "Probably not. There will be some marine life, but nothing like there is now."

I jumped off the couch. "We have to draw that!" I said. "It HAS to be part of our whole presentation to Mr. Drake!"

"I think you're right," Dad said.

Mom offered to take me to work with her the next day to see what I could find there that might help our case. For the first time, I was excited about going to my mom's lab. In the past I'd go if I had to. I'd just eat chips out of the vending machine and play computer games with Mom's scientist friends, but I never paid much attention to what anyone actually did there. This time would be different.

We made a plan. I'd go to work with Mom in the morning, and then Dad would pick us up for lunch.

When I called Tess to tell her that I couldn't be at the booth in the morning, she said, "That's OK.

My sister and I will handle it."

I thought I'd heard wrong.

"No, really," Tess giggled. "Dee will take me to the cove. She WANTS to help with the booth!"

I almost fell off my chair. "DEE?" I asked.

"Yeah," said Tess. "She thinks it sounds like a great way to meet guys."

• • •

When we got to Mom's lab, Mom showed me stuff on the computer that just looked like designs until she explained them to me. I knew about bar charts and pie charts and graphs from school, but these bars and points and lines were really colorful. They looked more like abstract art.

Mom explained that it was because they were measuring so many things at once. The lavender-to-purple bars were measuring the toxins diluting in the seawater, meaning poisonous stuff that was really totally awful right where it was dumped into the sea but that got less horrible as it mixed in with the water farther away. But the diluting wave was different from the dissolving wave, which was in shades of gray. The deep-blue-to-baby-blue lines were measuring oxygen. The entire rainbow was about temperature, and the green showed the density of living things. Blue green was plants, and yellow green was animals.

It was so cool to finally *get* what I was looking at. But then it was so UNcool, because now I understood that it was really bad news for the tide-pool creatures, because when human interference went up, marine life went way, way down.

Then Mom had her own work to do, so she left me to search for more information myself on her computer. I came across a Web site that blew me away. I'd heard the term "food chain" before, but I'd never really understood it. Now I do. It's the order of who eats who. And when just one link of the chain is taken away, the whole thing breaks. Like a chain on a bike.

Here's what I learned: The tiniest plants and animals that live on underwater rocks are a favorite snack food down there. So, once the littlest guys are gone, the medium-sized sea creatures who eat them have to either starve or go looking somewhere else for food. If those middle-sized ones leave, then the bigger ones (who eat the medium-sized ones) have to either follow them or starve . . . and on and on it goes, link by link in the chain. You take out one link, and the whole thing is wrecked.

And the chain goes the other way, too. Those tiny guys who live on the rocks eat algae. So when the rocks are gone, taking the little guys with them, the algae is left to grow and grow and grow all out of whack, until it's huge and chokes everything else out of the water. It's all about balance.

It turns out that our cove isn't the first or only place being destroyed for "recreational progress." That means that animals, and sometimes whole environments, are endangered or going extinct—not for medical research to cure diseases, not to create shelter for the homeless or raise food for the hungry. No, these innocent Mr. Crabbys are being wiped out just so people can zoom around in their speedboats and water bikes and jet skis for fun.

All this was pretty freaky. It was scaring and depressing me, but I was really proud I found it.

I also was really proud of my mom for working on such cool and important, life-and-death stuff. And to think I used to think her job was dull and boring!

Everyone at the lab was really nice to me, and I could tell that they looked up to my mom. That was cool. And when her boss shook my hand and said, "I can see that you have the makings of a true environmental activist," I felt great, even though I wasn't exactly sure what an activist was.

Afterward I asked Mom, and she said an activist is someone who works at making the world a better place, someone with the courage to act on her convictions, to stick to her principles in spite of the odds, and to take action!

"Anyone can hope things get better and wish problems would get solved," Mom added. "And anyone can grumble and complain about things. But an activist takes it upon herself to fight for improvement, to make the world a better place, to right wrongs, to correct mistakes, and to bring about change for the good." Then she smiled at me and said, "Like you."

Me? Me!

When Dad picked us up, he asked me about my morning and I said, "It was great and terrible."

That made him laugh.

Then I explained. "The great was that I learned so much. The terrible was this." I showed him the drawings of the dead ocean and explained the graphs and charts of sea life before and after other marinas had been built.

Dad nodded sadly, then he changed the subject to tell me his news: Mr. Luther Drake's secretary had called to set up their appointment for tomorrow morning! Ten o'clock. "Are you and Tess going to come with me?" Dad asked.

"Tomorrow? That's so SOON," I said.

Dad nodded. "Well, tomorrow's the day."

I thought about it all through lunch. I went back and forth in my mind between "Sure! It'll be great!" and "Oh no! We're nowhere near ready!"

As the minutes ticked by, my confidence melted away and I had fewer "Sure"s and more "Oh no"s. By the time we got to the beach, I was afraid the whole art protest idea stunk big-time. I felt more like a scared little girl than like an activist.

I got out of the car and saw Tess yawning, looking bored to death at our booth. Dee was tossing her hair, looking annoyed. The "Oh no"s were definitely way in the lead.

I walked over and started yanking the petals off the yellow dahlia Jeremy must have left. Dee snatched the flower out of my hands and stuck it back in the vase.

"It'll be fun!" Tess said after I told her about tomorrow. "We'll get dressed up and we'll carry in our stack of drawings and we'll say . . . I don't know what exactly, but we'll say something, that's for sure."

"By the way, what are we going to do about the people who drew for us before we got the draw-for-a-drawing idea?" I asked Tess.

Dee rolled her eyes, but Tess knew what I meant. "I guess we could tear the signatures off their pictures and throw them in the fishbowl. Just to be fair."

"But," I said, "not until after we've shown all the drawings to Julia's son-in-law. Right?"

"Right," Tess agreed.

"You two are so gorked," Dee said. I guess she hadn't met all the boys she thought she would, because she was back to her sour old self. "I'm outta here, losers," she said, and left.

Tess and I looked through the drawings. I was impressed by how many people could really draw. And it was cool that there were so many different ways to draw and still have it look like our cove. I thought that was nice until I remembered Dad saying that The Man would say, "There are plenty of fish in the sea, or artists in the town." Not that any of them were anywhere as good as my dad, but still . . .

"How many drawings do you think we have altogether?" Tess asked.

"Fifty-seven at last count," I said. "Plus the ones you got this morning. But what if Mr. Drake won't even look at our stuff? What if he's really mean?"

"What if he gets so mad that he won't let your dad do any of the hotel art?" Tess asked. "Won't your dad be awfully disappointed?"

I shrugged, getting more nervous by the second. "My dad said we could come," I reminded her and myself. "And he's not going to take this gig if they cart off the tide pools, so . . ." I shrugged again. "But it would be nice to be rich for a while. And all those paintings, plus two great big huge murals—how cool would that be?"

We both sighed.

I knew that the one thing that would calm me down would be to at least stick my feet in the ocean. I could climb down the cliff right there, behind our booth, and splash out into that cold, clean water. I closed my eyes and imagined it—the way it would shock my skin awake, the way it would tingle and pull.

I opened my eyes and looked at Tess's foot in its cast, propped up on the tree stump, and I said, "Maybe we'd better go home and look at what we've got. Plan our attack for tomorrow. Let's forget about getting any more drawings, OK?"

Tess said, "OK."

We called my dad over. He said it was fine with him to leave, because he was too nervous about tomorrow to concentrate today.

"Us too," I said. We loaded up the car to leave. But at the last second I told Tess and Dad to wait, and I ran to Jeremy's to tell him that tomorrow was the big day.

"Good luck, lovey!" he said. "My hopes fly with you!"

I ran across to the diner. I had to wait while Julia served a tuna melt and fries to a lady at the counter. Then I told Julia that we were going to see her son-in-law the next day. "Can you give me any tips about him?" I asked. "Like if he's a Padres fan or something, I could wear my Padres cap. Or if his favorite color is purple . . ."

But Julia couldn't think of anything. She just said, "Good luck, honey. You'll do fine."

• • •

It was a long afternoon and a longer night. When at last it was morning, Tess showed up at my house with her mom's famous lemon squares stacked prettily and wrapped in plastic with a yellow bow.

"My mom sent these for Mr. Drake," Tess said. "She figured it couldn't hurt."

"Mmmm!" my mom said. "Lynn's lemon squares! These will bring that Drake fellow to his senses."

Tess's mom had sent extras for me and my folks. Mom put hers in her lunch sack.

Dad said he was too nervous to eat.

I gobbled mine down so fast, I didn't even taste it. Then I ate Dad's.

Mom kissed all of us and made me promise that we'd call her at the lab the second our meeting was over. I watched her get on her bike and pedal away. *Bye, Mom.*

Dad was pacing round and round.

Tess and I went to my room.

We'd already counted the drawings; there were sixty-one. We were tempted to leave out the really babyish ones, like the campers' drawings and some restaurant kids' scribbles. But then we decided that wouldn't be right, because we'd told people their art would be part of our protest, and so it should be. And even little kids can help make a difference. At least we hoped so!

We agreed to show the kids' pictures first and

save the best for last: the scientific ones from Mom's lab next to last, then Julia's cartoon as the ultimate kicker.

"Do you think Mr. Drake will be really scary?" Tess asked. "Like, do you think he'll yell at us?"

I shrugged. "The guy is a tide-pool destroyer," I said. "How nice can he be?"

I wished we'd had longer to plan.

I wished I'd never started this.

Tess said she wished I'd shut up.

I said I wished it was already over.

Tess said she wished she'd worn her blue skirt.

When Dad knocked on my bedroom door and said, "It's time, girls," I wished he was talking to someone else.

Tess and I held hands in the car.

I expected Mr. Drake's office to be all fancy, but it was in a cozy bungalow on a cul-de-sac. His receptionist explained apologetically that he wasn't there yet. She offered us coffee or tea.

We all said, "No thanks."

We sat down in the waiting room, trying to look straight-backed and professional, but the couch was so squishy, we sank. We watched the door, waiting in nervous silence. Dad had a portfolio of his work. I had our stack of drawings and the lemon squares. Tess had her crutches.

Then a man came bursting in, all huffy and puffy, his hair wet, shirt open, necktie flapping untied.

"Sorry I'm late," he said, shifting his coffee cup and jacket and briefcase to try to free a hand to shake with Dad. "Come on in!" he said. "I'm so glad to finally meet you. I'm a big fan of your work."

Tess and I looked at each other.

Mr. Drake noticed us and smiled. "Are these young ladies with you?" he asked Dad.

Dad nodded, still speechless. Then he managed to croak out an introduction. I'd never seen Dad so nervous in my entire life.

"Well, nice to meet you, Kailey and Tess," said

Mr. Drake. "Come on in." And he led us into his office.

The first thing I noticed was the wall of photos. There were dozens—all of the same two kids. Picture after picture after picture of them smiling, crying, dressed up in party clothes, and in costumes, and in pajamas. Eating, sleeping, sitting on Santa's lap, riding tricycles, swinging on swings, flying kites . . .

"Wow!" I said.

He smiled. "Daria and Theo," he said. "My Daria is three and a half and my Theo is two."

I said, "They're cute."

Mr. Drake smiled even more. Then he gestured at his couch and chairs and said, "Please, have a seat."

We sat. These chairs were less squishy, luckily.

This is the evil covekiller? I thought. *This is the guy who wants to cart away an entire tide-pool colony?* I glanced over at Tess to see if she was thinking the same thing I was, but her face was a total blank.

I looked at Dad. He was expressionless, too. They were both scared stiff!

I turned my attention back to Mr. Drake, cleared my throat, and asked him if his children liked the beach.

"Oh yes!" he said. "I take them whenever I can."

"Have you ever shown them the tide pools?" I asked.

"They're still a little young to appreciate that," he laughed.

"I was as young as they are when I started going," I said. "It's been my favorite place for as long as I can remember. I always loved to peek in at all the little creatures and watch them living their tiny lives. It's really cool, and it's way more interesting than TV."

I stopped to breathe and hoped I didn't sound weird and pushy. But it was too late to worry about that now.

"You should definitely take your kids," I said. "I swear they'll love it. In fact, we have drawings of the tide pools done by some artists who are no older than Daria and Theo!"

Mr. Drake looked confused. So I showed him.

And while he looked through the drawings, I tried to explain why we'd collected them. I kept shooting looks at Dad and Tess until finally they found their voices and helped a little. Our explanation wasn't very clear and we interrupted each other some, but I was pretty sure Mr. Drake got our point.

His face worried up when he looked at my mom's science stuff. And he smiled a little when he got to Julia's cartoon. When I told him who had drawn it, he looked confused.

"Julia? My mother-in-law?" he asked.

When I nodded, he looked at it again and laughed. But it was the kids' drawings that really seemed to catch his interest. He turned back to them and flipped through again and again.

"The whole reason I want to build the marina," he said, "is for my children. For Theodore and Daria."

"I'm sure they'd like it," I said, "with boats and all that. But there are already plenty of places for boats along the coast. How many places have tide pools?"

"With excellent snorkeling," Tess managed
to whisper.

"They add enormously to the drama and majesty
of the cove," Dad said, "speaking as an artist."

"And they're a blast," I added, "speaking as a kid.
Plus, they are living things," I said, "speaking as an
environmental activist." I surprised even myself by
saying that, and I expected Tess to laugh at me or
poke me, or Dad to raise his eyebrows at least, but
neither of them did anything.

"The rocks aren't living, of course," I went on.
"But all the animals and plants that need the rocks
are. And that's why we're here, because the tide-pool
creatures cannot speak up for themselves."

"We're excited about the movies, though!" Tess
managed to say in a fairly normal tone of voice. "And
my sister is practically holding her breath until the
shops open," she smiled.

I jumped in to say, "Tess is right. The whole

resort thing sounds great."

"Fantabulous!" Tess agreed.

"It's just the beach we're talking about. The rocks. The tide pools."

Mr. Luther Drake nodded thoughtfully for a while. Then he turned his attention to my dad and said, "I was hoping to discuss your commission for the paintings. But I suspect there's a connection between the two topics. Am I correct? Rocks and paintings?"

Dad swallowed hard. "Yes," he said, sounding more like himself. "There is an unbreakable connection between the cove rocks and my paintings."

"I see," Mr. Drake said.

Dad fidgeted with his portfolio. Then he said, "I'm enormously flattered by your interest in my work, and I thank you for that. But as much as I'd love to do those paintings for your resort, I couldn't in clear conscience be a part of anything that would destroy the natural beauty of our cove."

Mr. Drake tilted back in his chair. "I see," he said again.

No one said anything for what seemed like a long, long time. Then Mr. Drake stood up and stuck his hand out at my dad, saying, "Thank you so much for coming down here today. I appreciate your taking the time."

Dad jumped to his feet and shook Mr. Drake's hand. "My pleasure," Dad said.

Tess and I got up, too. I didn't know about her, but I felt like crying. I put the plate of lemon squares on Mr. Drake's desk and said, "These are for you."

He smiled. "Well, thank you very much," he said, and bowed to me a little. I sort of bowed back, and then we left.

When we got into the car, I said, "I don't get it. Did I miss something back there?"

Dad shrugged. "I'm not sure," he said, "but I think we just got thrown out."

"Politely, though," Tess said.

Dad nodded. "Yes, very politely."

"So, was he nice or not?" I wailed. "I'm all confused! He smiled and was so friendly and then—bam! We're back in the car."

"Just like that, eighty-eight paintings and two murals—out the window," Dad muttered, shaking his head. "Amazing."

I felt awful. I remembered that I'd promised to call Mom, but I sure didn't want to.

Dad finally started the car and pulled away from the curb. "Anyone hungry?" he asked.

I said, "No."

But Tess said, "Starved."

How could she be starved? Just the idea of food made me seasick.

Dad drove to the diner and I thought, *Ick.* I hoped Julia wouldn't be there, but it seemed like it was always her shift. And I knew Jeremy would spot us and come flying over to hear the story. *Ick, ick, ick!* I just wanted to crawl into a cave and hide—like Mr. Crabby.

But there was nowhere to hide. We tromped into the diner and did not get the bay-window table because someone else was there. The counter was taken, too. Figures. We took another table and stared at the menu.

Julia showed up with our waters and said, "So, what time is your meeting with Luther?"

"We already had it," I said.

She said, "Oh."

Then she must've noticed our gloomy faces because she said, "You all look like you could use the breakfast special. Two buttermilk jacks, two eggs any way you like them, two strips of bacon, two sausages, and a glass of OJ." Julia smiled. "Sound right?"

"Yes!" Tess said. "That sounds great!"

"Thanks, Julia," said Dad, "but coffee and wheat toast will be fine for me."

All I could do was shake my head a little.

Jeremy has either a nose like a hound dog or

eyes like a hawk, or he'd been watching out the window all morning, because as soon as we'd ordered, in he came carrying two orange zinnias. He rushed over to our table and handed one to me and one to Tess, saying, "Tell me! Are these zinnias of celebration?"

Tess said, "'Fraid not. They're sympathy flowers."

We tried to explain what had happened at our meeting, although none of us was actually sure what did happen.

When the food came, I couldn't even look in Tess's direction as she chomped and splashed through her mountain of food. I couldn't see out the bay window from our table, so I looked across the room at Dad's painting. I tried telling myself that our cove was just a teeny part of the whole long coastline. So, even if our cove was ruined, there would still be the great big gigantic ocean out there, with miles of tide pools and beaches. I told myself that Mr. Crabby and the rest of the tide-pool creatures and I would find each other somewhere else.

Then Tess kicked me hard with her good foot. My head spun around in time to see Mr. Luther Drake walk in the door of the diner with a big old grin on his face.

"That's him!" I hissed to Jeremy. Then we all just froze, watching him come toward us. Suddenly he was towering over our table, and we said "Hi" in nervous, squeaky little voices.

"May I join you?" he asked, and we all sprang to life, shoving chairs aside, moving plates and glasses. Julia beelined over to our table and swatted Mr. Drake on the head with her order pad.

I'm sure it didn't really hurt, but he said, "Ouch, Ma, cut it out!" and smiled. "I just came to tell these nice people that those were the best lemon squares I have ever tasted in my entire life. The absolute, undisputed best. And THAT from a man who truly admires lemon squares perhaps above all other desserts."

"My mom made them," Tess said.

"Ah!" Mr. Drake said. "Then your mother is a truly gifted woman, and you are a very lucky child."

Tess giggled, but I was too nervous to join her.

"And if there's one thing lemon squares do," Mr. Drake continued, "it's make me rethink things."

Julia lifted her pad as if to smack him again and said, "Stop torturing these nice people and tell them what you came to say!"

Luther Drake made a show of cowering away from his mother-in-law and said, "I'm getting to that."

Tess was giggling out of control now, and I saw Dad's lips twitch into an almost-smile. Not me, though.

"I'm a man who truly appreciates perfection," Mr. Drake said. "That's why I knew I had to marry Julia's daughter Connie the second I laid eyes on her."

That made Julia put the order pad back in her pocket.

Mr. Drake continued, "That's also why I want you, Pete, to do the paintings for my resort, so my guests will not only have perfect service and perfect accommodations, but they'll also have"—he pointed to Dad's painting—"the perfect art on the walls."

I heard Dad take in a deep breath.

Mr. Drake smiled at my dad, and then nodded at me and Tess, saying, "And of course, as you girls so wisely and creatively pointed out, the perfect view is absolutely essential."

"I've been telling you that all along!" Julia said.

"That's true, you have," he said. "I hope you'll forgive me, but it didn't make PERFECT sense until I thought about the presentation these clever girls made. This had been one of my pet projects, and my goal was to make an ideal place for my kids to take their holidays. I'd thought the perfect view would be a marina—gleaming white docks, bright white sails against the blue sea, scrubbed decks, masts in the sky."

"Sounds pretty," Tess said. I wanted to kick her, but I didn't.

"It is indeed, and there are hundreds of places

where Daria and Theo can have that view. But our own stretch of unspoiled coast—complete with those amazing tide pools I just went to see—now that's getting rarer every day!"

"Fantabulous!" said Tess.

Everyone was smiling and I wanted to, too, but I needed to be really sure. I needed him to say it right out, not talk around it or hint. "So," I said, "are you saying you're not going to build the marina?"

"Yes," he said, "that's what I'm saying."

Tess, Dad, Jeremy, and Julia cheered and hugged.

"And you're not going to destroy the tide pools or dredge the shore?" I asked.

"That's right," he said.

"You're sure?" I asked.

Mr. Drake put his hand out and said, "Perfectly sure!" And he and I shook hands on it. From then on, breakfast was one big party! Mr. Drake even said we could raffle off a weekend stay at his resort for the people who'd entered our drawing.

"Well, then I'm going to enter MY name in the contest!" Tess said.

"No need for that," Mr. Drake said. "I'd be delighted to have you two girls and your families as my guests one weekend."

"Guests like meaning FREE?" Tess asked.

"Perfectly free," he answered.

Tess and I squealed, and I said, "Oh, Mr. Drake, thank you so much!"

He said, "You're welcome, as long as you call me Luther instead of Mr. Drake."

Then I remembered, "We've got to call Mom!"

Mr. Drake handed me his cell phone and I dialed the lab. Mom answered on the first ring, but then I got shy about telling her in front of Mr. Drake—I mean Luther.

"Hi, Mom," I said. "How are you?"

"How am I?" she asked. "You're asking how *I* am? WHAT HAPPENED, for Pete's sake?"

I started to laugh.

"Kailey, tell me!" Mom said.

But I handed the phone to Dad to explain while I let myself laugh and laugh and laugh it all out—until tears trickled down my cheeks.

• • •

The next morning, Dad took me to the beach on the way to Tess's house. Down I went, straight out to the tide pools. I bent over and looked in at the calm, sparkly little world of one pool that had a bunch of barnacles and a tiny starfish in it. Another pool was full of sea anemones waving their tentacles. A crab, maybe even the very same Mr. Crabby, walked sideways across the rock, pincers up.

"Hi, guys," I said.

Only the wind and the sound of the surf answered.

"I kept my promise," I said. "See?"
A wave came up—WHOOSH—and soaked me to the skin from head to toe. I sputtered and laughed and spit out salt water. And I knew that everything was going to be all right. Surf's up!

True
Story

Meet Talia, an American girl
who, like Kailey, loves to surf
and wants to protect tide pools
so that everyone—people and sea
animals alike—can enjoy them.

When Talia Hancock moved to Southern California, she took up a new hobby—surfing—right away. It wasn't easy at first; it took her two days of practicing over and over before she was able to stand upright on a surfboard and ride a wave. But once she got the hang of it, she was hooked. "The best part is when the ride begins, and the wave first starts to pull you," says Talia. "I also love just sitting out there on the ocean, with a friend or with my brothers, waiting for the next wave."

On shore, Talia found another new love—tide pools. Doheny State Beach is not far from Talia's house, so she goes there often. "At Doheny there's lots of little tide pools and one huge tidepool that kids can paddle around in," Talia says. "The big tidepool has tons of animals. Hermit crabs and sea slugs are my favorites, but there are lots of other animals—mussels, anemones, sea stars, urchins, and

Sea Urchin

Hermit Crab

limpets. By carefully turning over a few rocks and looking in shells, I find these incredibly interesting creatures."

Watching a tide pool is like peeking into a little world. Talia spends hours exploring tide pools and observing the animals up close. So when her seventh-grade science teacher announced the Young Naturalists Award given every year by the American Museum of Natural History in New York, Talia decided to submit an essay and drawings about tide-pool life. A few months later, the museum e-mailed

For her essay, Talia drew the anemone, sea urchin, and hermit crab on this page, as well as the crab on page 146.

her to inform her that she was a finalist. Her class was very excited! But more time passed, and Talia figured she hadn't won. So she was completely surprised when she got a phone call from the museum telling her she had won an all-expenses-paid trip to New York City to receive the award!

Talia is glad that the tide pools at Doheny Beach are protected by being in a state park, but she knows that other tide pools face threats from developers eager to build on scenic beachfront property. And all tide pools can be damaged by pollution, such as oil spills and garbage. Even at Doheny, says Talia, "there's a run-off reservoir right next to the tide pools that's totally polluted. When it gets full, it dumps out onto the beach, and then the water isn't safe for swimming. People accept this because they're used to it, but I think it's wrong to put bad stuff in the ocean—not only where animals live but where people and kids are swimming."

The life within a tide pool may seem like a separate world apart from us, but, as Talia notes, "what we do affects the tide pool too."

Tide-pool Tips

Tide-pool creatures are specially adapted to survive rough waves, scouring sand, hot sun, and hungry seagulls. They're good at camouflage and hiding under rocks. To find them, sit beside a pool for a few minutes and watch quietly as animals begin to move around. You can even touch them gently. Follow these guidelines to protect the tide pools—and yourself—as you explore.

- Wear shoes that can get wet and won't slip easily.
- Go with an older friend or an adult.
- Low tide is the best time for viewing. But keep an eye on the ocean—don't let the rising tide cut off your route back to shore.
- Avoid stepping on tide-pool creatures such as barnacles, mussels, or sea urchins.
- If you pick up an animal, put it back right where you found it.
- Don't put anything else into a tide pool, such as a coin or food—it could poison the animals.
- Never pry animals or plants off rocks. This will injure or kill them.

Visit a Virtual Tide Pool

Landlocked? These Web sites let you tour tide pools without getting your toes wet.

- Meet the animals you might find in a California tide pool at
  http://bonita.mbnms.nos.noaa.gov/Visitor/Tidepool/

- Enjoy great shots of girls and tide pools, as well as beautiful pictures of ocean animals, at this professional photographer's Web site.
  http://www.richardherrmann.com/tidepool.htm

Kailey

About the Author

Amy Goldman Koss wrote the AG Fiction titles *Stolen Words* and *Smoke Screen*. She wishes she lived as close to the beach as her character Kailey does. She'd love to be able to poke around in the tide pools any old time. But the mountains are nice, too. Instead of starfish, she has deer and bobcat in her neighborhood!